O9-BUB-298

# THE REDHEADED PRINCESS

*The*
# REDHEADED
# PRINCESS

A NOVEL

*Ann Rinaldi*

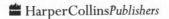 HarperCollins*Publishers*

www.harpercollinschildrens.com

Library of Congress Cataloging-in-Publication Data

Rinaldi, Ann.

The redheaded princess / Ann Rinaldi. — 1st ed.

p.   cm.

Summary: In 1542, nine-year-old Lady Elizabeth lives on an estate near
London, striving to get back into the good graces of her father, King Henry VIII,
and as the years pass she faces his death and those of other close relatives until
she finds herself next in line to ascend the throne of England in 1558.

ISBN-13: 978-0-06-073374-2 (trade bdg.)

ISBN-13: 978-0-06-073375-9 (lib. bdg.)

1. Elizabeth I, Queen of England, 1533–1603—Childhood and youth—
Juvenile fiction. 2. Great Britain—History—Elizabeth, 1558–1603—Juvenile
fiction. [1. Elizabeth I, Queen of England, 1533–1603—Childhood and youth—
Fiction. 2. Great Britain—History—Elizabeth, 1558–1603—Fiction.
3. Princesses—Fiction. 4. Kings, queens, rulers, etc.—Fiction.] I. Title.

PZ7.R459Red 2008                                              2007018577

[Fic]—dc22                                                          CIP

                                                                         AC

Typography by Amy Ryan

2 3 4 5 6 7 8 9 10

❖

First Edition

*To our own little princess*
*and first granddaughter,*
*Nicole Ann Rinaldi*

❧

# Read This First

The year is 1542. Young Elizabeth, the second daughter of King Henry VIII of England, is only nine years old. She is living at Hatfield, one of her father's estates, which is modern, commodious, lovely with gardens and a deer park, and only twenty miles from London.

Her nanny, Catherine "Cat" Ashley, and her "household" live with her. Her household consists of knights, squires, those who tend and keep the gardens and animals, housemaids, and tutors, as well as those who manage her estate. She has always known that at her birth she was declared heir to the Crown.

But she has been living in exile from her father, who removed her from the line of succession and endorsed an act of Parliament declaring both her and her half sister, Mary, illegitimate.

Since she was three years old, Elizabeth has feared death. Death is all around her all the time. And the person who most represents that is her father, who had her mother, Anne Boleyn, beheaded when Elizabeth was three years old, as well as his fifth wife, Catherine Howard. Elizabeth has witnessed the "sweating sickness," which can come in an instant and wipe out a whole village. Life is tenuous at best, she decides. She is always afraid.

But she is also brave, industrious, and scholarly. At four she learned Latin from Cat Ashley. She has world-renowned tutors who teach her Italian, French, Hebrew, all about Rome and Cicero, Aesop's fables, science, and penmanship. Her dearest childhood friend is Robert "Robin" Dudley, son of John Dudley, Duke of Northumberland, who is of prominence in her father's court. She and Robin have long talks and ride horses together, and he is her sworn friend for all of her life.

Elizabeth has fair skin, dark eyes, and exquisite reddish hair, as well as beautiful hands with slender, long fingers. She resembles her father, not her mother. Always she is aware that she is being groomed to rule England someday, even though the idea of a female on the throne is repugnant to many, and up to now she has been in disgrace because of her mother.

Her father's one misery is that he did not have more sons. He cast aside his first wife, Catherine of Aragon, because she gave him only a daughter (Elizabeth's half sister, Mary). Breaking from Rome and the Roman Catholic Church, in an unprecedented action, he started his own

Church of England and divorced Catherine to marry Elizabeth's mother, Anne Boleyn. Then he had her beheaded for adultery. His third wife was Jane Seymour, who gave him a son, Edward, born in 1537. Jane died soon after childbirth, and King Henry contracted to marry Anne of Cleves, whom he imported to be his fourth wife. But he "liked her not" and very soon set her aside too and ever after treated her like a sister.

Next he wed Catherine Howard, a cousin of Ann Boleyn's. Like her cousin, Catherine was beheaded for adultery.

He is now about to marry Katharine Parr, the daughter of Sir Thomas Parr, the master of his household.

Katharine Parr is determined to bring Elizabeth, Mary, and Edward—all the king's children—together so they may act as a family.

Elizabeth trusts no one. She may want to, but she has learned not to. But although she is wary of marriage, seeing all her father's marriages fail, she keeps an open mind about Katharine Parr. As for her father, she is confused about him, aspiring to be like him one minute and afraid of him the next. She wants to be Queen someday, yet there are so many obstacles in her pathway. Now comes the summons she most fears and hopes for. Her father, the King, wants her to come to the palace.

PROLOGUE

One thing I have learned in this life: It is never good when you hear a horse galloping up to your home in the middle of the day or night. Night is worse, of course. Everything is worse at night, especially when you have no mother. The nights are filled with terror anyway, if you have no mother.

The rider who gallops the horse means you no good. Good news can always wait, I have discovered. Bad news must be delivered instantly, lest it consume the messenger, who fears for his life just because he is bringing it.

That's the way all the bad news in my life came to me. The news that my mother was executed, when I was only three, though there are those who say I cannot recollect that. The news when I was nine that I was no longer to be called Princess Elizabeth, but Lady Elizabeth, because my father had practically disowned me. All brought by messengers on galloping horses in the middle of the night.

*When I am Queen someday,* I would tell myself, *when I am Queen I will allow no more of these messengers to come in the middle of the night. If they must come, they must wait until morning, when the sun is out and shining, so their long faces don't look so dark and their black, musty clothes don't look so threatening.*

Or better yet, *When I am Queen there will be no more bad news. Ever.*

## CHAPTER ONE

*O*f course I knew I couldn't be Queen. No woman could ever rule over men in England. I had known that since I was three years old. But for days on end, I would sometimes pretend I was Queen. I would order about the rest of my household in what everyone knew was a game. I'd order about my knights, James and Richard Vernon, who were sons of a local squire, and Sir John Chertsey, a young knight of the shire. They were most faithful to me and out of earshot of my nurse, Cat Ashley, would call me Your Highness.

If Cat Ashley caught me, she would scold. "Pretending you are Queen is a dangerous game," she'd say, and then to the knights who were kneeling about me, "and you should know better than to encourage her."

So I'd pretend I was a witch. They say my mother, Anne Boleyn, was a witch. She had the tiniest hint of a sixth finger on her left hand, truly the sign of a witch. And she had special long sleeves attached to her gowns to try to hide it. So it became a fashion to have such a gown and the whole palace of women wanted such. And then there is the way they say she bewitched my father, not wanting to become his mistress like every other woman in court, but staying distant enough to drive him mad while she held out for marriage.

When Cat Ashley caught me at that game, she decided I should have lessons in behavior in case I was summoned to court. I must learn to kneel at my father's feet, to look him square in the eye, to show him I was fearless, yet be respectful at the same time.

"He hates cowardly children," she told me.

Besides my dear friend Robin Dudley, whom I saw only on occasion, I didn't have many playmates. There was my half brother, Edward, to be sure, but he was still a baby. Cousin Jane Grey was a mousy little creature, always reading her Bible and praying. She shirked at playing archery or quoits or any outdoor game at all. She hated horseback riding, which I loved.

My half sister, Mary, was seventeen years older than I and was appointed to attend me for a while because she and her mother (who had been put aside for my mother) were out of favor. But that was a royal failure. There Mary was, at seventeen, and her household was broken up around her and she was brought to Hatfield to wait upon me. What followed I do not much recall, but they tell me she refused to call me Princess or curtsey to me. She refused to eat. She spent hours in her room crying. Our father, in turn, took away her jewels. But with determination worthy of our lionhearted father, she won. She would wait on me and play with me, but she won because she never called me Princess and never curtseyed to me.

Finally she was relieved of her job, and things have never been the same between us since.

Only Robin Dudley was my true friend. Oh, the rides we have had together! Even at nine we were both experts with horses. He was frequently allowed to visit me at Hatfield, and the few times I went to court he was there, smoothing the way of things for me.

My clothing, while I was growing up at Hatfield, was on the shabby side. My father never sent fabrics for proper attire. Frequently Cat Ashley would write to court to beg an allowance or some fabric to dress me as I was supposed to be dressed. But there was never any response, and she had to make do with what she had. Somehow she always kept a special dress for me for in case I was summoned to court. Many were outgrown before they were used. But we always had to be ready.

I had been to court as a baby, I was told, and then again when I was four for the christening of my brother, Edward. At that time I was too young to take part in the procession and had to be carried by Sir Thomas Seymour.

Sir Thomas was brother to Jane Seymour, who was my brother Edward's mother. He was so dashing, so handsome. Every woman at court was in love with him. Even at four, I was too. I sensed this man was special, a courtier for all seasons. I have been in love with him ever since, and every time I go to court I hope to see him, but I am not always so fortunate.

Here is a puzzle. They are saying that Sir Thomas is in love with Katharine Parr, who is now to wed my father. But once my father claimed his right with her, Sir Thomas wouldn't even dance with her at court anymore. Not because he was angry, but because they were both afraid the King would suspect their love. Sir Thomas knows he has no rights to Katharine Parr while the King claims her, so he keeps his distance. Oh, isn't that a romantic story? It gives me the chills.

When I was seven, I went back to court again, for my father married Catherine Howard, my cousin, who was just eighteen. I loved Catherine. Her clothes were in the French fashion and my father gave her many jewels. She was young and frivolous and my father was besotted with her. And she spoiled me and gave me many presents.

But one day, when she and her ladies were practicing dancing, the guards came and told her: "It is no more time to dance." And they took her away. Because my father had been told she had committed adultery.

It is her beheading that haunts me more than my

mother's. When my mother was beheaded, I was too young even to know what it meant. Or what a horrible way it was to die. I remember being told how Catherine fought her guards when she was bundled into the boat to be taken to the Tower of London to await execution. They said she wore a black velvet dress and on the way to the Tower the boat passed London Bridge, where the heads of two of her young male lovers were impaled. Francis Dereham and Thomas Culpeper had both "played the King false" with her. They had suffered much, being tortured before death.

It was February 1542, cold and bone chilling when she went to the block. Robin told me about it. Robin hugged me when I cried. For I was crying for my mother as well as Catherine Howard.

The summons came when I was nine to go to court again.

I loved the journey to Whitehall Palace. I traveled in a litter surrounded by my people, yeomen of the guard, my knights, my serving maids, Cat Ashley, and Mr. Parry, keeper of my monies.

The most we made was six miles a day and the people came out all along the way to see us pass, to throw kisses and flowers, to see the horses dressed so magnificently, the wagons with my supplies, and me.

These were the local people, the poor farming people, the people who suffered when the plague of sweating sickness came, the people who knew what a bad harvest or a war could do to them. They saw hope in me, I suppose. They saw my flaming red hair. They knew I looked like my father. They prayed I would be like him. And that someday I would be Queen.

They were not like the upper classes, who saw a woman on the throne as an aberration against nature, who thought that a woman's mind was not good enough to think as a ruler, who thought that the first thing a woman should do on becoming Queen was to marry some prince to rule in her stead.

These people wanted nothing to do with a man ruling who was not born to it. Likely they were counting on the fact that if I ever became Queen, I would not wed a foreign prince. They knew the House of Tudor, to which I belonged, had ruled England successfully since 1485, when Henry Tudor had invaded England. To them this was not history. It was their life story, and they saw it continuing on in the form of a little girl with flaming red hair.

"God save you, Princess Elizabeth," they cried. And they came as close as my knights allowed, offering cakes and sweetmeats and singing songs.

I was not supposed to be called Princess. If they knew it they didn't care. Or mayhap they knew it and wanted me to know I was their Princess anyway.

And so we traveled. From Hatfield to Eastcote, from Wild Hill to Woodside, from Bell Bar to Waterend, from Mimms Street to Green Street.

Whitehall! The largest palace in Europe! Thanks to my

father, who had seized it when it was known as York Place from Thomas Wolsey, Archbishop of York, and made it his London home. It covered twenty-three acres on the Thames River. To build it, my father had to have hundreds of smaller homes demolished. It has gardens, courts, galleries. On the east side are the royal apartments.

My mother had been the first one to occupy the Queen's apartments. And now here came I.

But in no royal presence. By the time we got to Whitehall, the day's darkness had fallen and I was asleep. I awoke to Cat's soft murmurings, to see lighted torches all around me and the Royal Guard lined up in their red coats, to hear my knights giving orders, to feel the sniffings and licks of the palace dogs.

Then Richard Vernon took my hand to help me out of the litter and whispered, "Come along, Princess; you belong here."

I was both awed and frightened. The hugeness of the place belittled me. I feared my father and all these trappings of power. The great windows of the palace were ablaze with light. From an open doorway came a shout. "Make way for the Lady Elizabeth."

Richard and James Vernon escorted me inside.

I was half asleep. What was I to do? Would I meet my father this night? I stumbled and near fell on a doorstep, and Richard Vernon picked me up and carried me in his arms. I remember holding tightly on to him and hiding my face in his shoulder.

He carried me upstairs through arched corridors ablaze with torchlight. In the distance, in darkened rooms, I saw shapes, servants scurrying about and bowing. Then we went upstairs to the royal apartments, to my suite of rooms.

They were lavishly furnished, with tapestry bed hangings, artwork on the walls, sweetened rushes on the floor, and a fire burning cheerfully in the hearth. "Put her on the bed," Cat Ashley directed.

Servants brought a repast of pigeon pie and hot mulled wine and sweet wafers, but I was not hungry.

"I want to sleep," I told Cat.

"And so you shall." She hunted about in my trunks for my nightdress.

"Did you see all the people come out to greet me?"

"I did."

"They called me Princess."

"And you should never repeat it."

"Will you be here tomorrow?" I asked the Vernon brothers.

They assured me they would, and left the room. In the next moment I was struggling into my nightdress, and then in my bed wondering, Was this the room my mother once occupied? Was her ghost still about? What would I do if I saw it?

I waited, but it never came. I went to sleep.

CHAPTER TWO

*T*he next morning when I awoke, I knew somehow that something was wrong. The early-morning sounds in the palace were missing. There were no maids giggling and whispering. No rustling of skirts in the corridor or barked orders from the commander of the guards.

True, I had not been here since Katharine had married my father a few months back. We children had not been invited. It had been a private wedding in the Queen's closet at Hampton Court. Mayhap, I thought as I ate the breakfast Cat brought me, mayhap Katharine sleeps late and likes a quiet palace. "What's amiss?" I asked Cat. "Why is this place so quiet, and why is everybody moping about?"

"Wrong? Nothing. You should dress now to meet your father. I want you to wear your very best green."

Green was my color, she said, given the red of my hair. So I dressed. And while she arranged my hair, pulling it back from my face so my profile was at its best, we talked.

"I like Katharine but I scarce know her," I said.

She arranged a white cap adorned with pearls on my head. "Well, you know she's been widowed before. The first husband was sixty-three and she only fourteen. She has lived in castles and even owns one. She inherited it from her second husband along with many riches. There, this cap is lovely, isn't it?"

"What else?" I asked.

She fixed my starched white uplifted collar. "She's lovely. She's written two books. She yearns for more education, and let's see. When your father had her friend Anne Askew executed for being a heretic, she said not a word."

My eyes went wide. "I heard about that. She was supposed to be burned at the stake but died quickly because a kind executioner lighted a bag of gunpowder that hung about her neck."

"Shh. We don't speak of such things," she admonished. "That's all gossip."

Gossip was the lifeblood of a palace, as everyone knew. Just as we knew that the people who knew about gossip first were the servants.

I stood up. "Do you think my father will like me in this?" I asked.

My dress was green damask banded with cloth of gold. "Your manners are more important than clothes," Cat said.

"But yes, he will like you. How can he not? You look much like him."

As I walked through the halls, past guards and maids and ambassadors, to wait outside the presence chamber, I thought about Katharine, now wed to my father. I knew him to be fifty-two and, they said, very fat. "As fat as no man needs to be," they said. And I knew about his sore leg. It was from an old wound and festered all the time now and he was in great pain. Only Katharine knew how to treat the leg. And then I thought, *She has to be a good person to be able to keep my father as she is keeping him.*

Outside the presence chamber I met Robin, my old friend, now a sturdy boy of nine and a whole head taller than I.

He kissed my hand and bowed. "My Lady Elizabeth," he said in all somberness.

"Robin." I giggled and put my arms around him. "You've gotten so tall."

"I'm about the business of growing up," he said. And he flashed a smile that showed even, white teeth. "And so are you, I see."

"How does all go with you, Robin?" I asked.

"Better now that I'm in your lovely presence."

"Ah, I see you're practicing to be a courtier," I said.

"A few more years and I'll match my wits with the best of them. Will you go riding with me after meeting with your father?"

"If I'm still able to breathe."

"You're that afraid of him?"

"Wouldn't you be?"

"I see you're trembling. You must try to contain yourself. Don't let him see your fear. It'll all be fine. I'm told he loves you."

"Oh, if only I could be sure of that, Robin."

"Be sure of it. Look, I'm off to pick the horses in the stables. Tell me, why do you look so sad, Elizabeth?"

"I don't know. It seems awfully somber around here this morning. Don't you sense it? Everybody is creeping around and nobody wants to meet my eyes. What is it, Robin? I'm frightened."

"Nothing for you to be frightened about. It's Katharine who should be frightened."

I felt a sense of dread. "Why?"

"She's been accused by the King and his council of being a wanton."

"A wanton?"

"Yes, and don't tell me you don't know what that means, Elizabeth. She's been accused of dallying with other men before she wed your father."

"She was married to two other men before she met my father."

"Nevertheless, her reputation is in shreds."

That's what was missing. That's what was wrong. On my last visit to the palace, though I did not really get to know her, I couldn't help noticing how Katharine spread cheer, talking about events to come, welcoming us children to the table with my father. There had even been talk of her getting me a private tutor now that Cat Ashley had taught me all she had to teach me.

Now silence echoed in the rooms. The vast hallways mocked me.

"Where is she?" I asked him.

"Confined to her chambers. The King is at mass. She wants to see him, one more time before . . ."

"Before what?" My voice trembled.

"Before they take her to the Tower. But he won't see her. He knows, they say, that if he does, he'll relent; he still loves her so. And everyone is saying it's just like the other time."

"The other time?" My voice broke. "They mean my mother, don't they? He's going to have her beheaded, like my mother?"

Robin didn't answer. I pushed past him and ran up the great stairway that led to the upper chambers. I knew where Katharine's apartments were, at the end of the hall. And already, as I became aware of the situation, I heard her crying and screaming and banging the door of her apartments, yelling to be let out.

Four members of the Royal Guard stood outside the door.

"Make way," one of them said, "for Lady Elizabeth."

This was before they realized what I was about. I ran to the door and grabbed the gold knob. One of the guards stepped forward and tried to stop me. "Lady Elizabeth," he said, "you don't want to go in there."

I felt the pearls shaking on my hood as I confronted him. "Yes, I do. I want to see Katharine."

"It isn't allowed, Lady." He gripped his halberd, his only weapon. He looked distraught. How could he go against the wishes of the nine-year-old daughter of the King? I knew I had my royalty in my favor.

"Stand back," I ordered him, in my best imperial voice.

The poor man was so confused he stood back. So did his companions. Then with one firm grasp, I opened the door.

I nearly fell into Katharine's arms.

"Elizabeth!" she shouted in surprise.

"Go," I said, "run."

She did, down the hall. The chapel was at the end and she ran screaming, "Henry, Henry, just see me this one time, my dear husband. Oh, Henry!" Her slippers flapped, her gown trailed out behind her.

She was wearing an underskirt of cloth of gold beneath a sleeved overdress of brocade lined with crimson satin. Around her neck was a large gold cross, studded with diamonds.

Outside the chapel doors stood four more guards with halberds raised. The guards who were behind me stood frozen, not knowing what to do. I blocked their way and they could not very well wrestle with the Lady Elizabeth, could they?

Katharine reached the chapel doors and managed to pound on them. In a few moments they opened and my father, the King, stood there in all his bulky magnificence, clad in orange and russet velvet trimmed with ermine, dangling his jewelry of state. On his head was his little sideways hat with a peacock feather twirled around toward his face. His leg was bandaged.

Immediately Katharine fell to her knees, begging for her life.

"By God, someone shall pay for this. Who let her out?" my father roared.

Silence from everyone.

"Can't I trust a living soul to do my bidding? Take her away. Take her back. Now."

Then he saw me at the other end of the hall, surrounded by four guards. "By heaven, you go too far," he roared again. "Do you think to put yourself above the thinking of your King?"

Katharine was brought back, weeping, half dragged by the guards. They took her past me into her apartments and closed the door. And at the top of the stairway, where I'd just come up, stood Robin and Cat Ashley. My saviors. If ever I needed them, I needed them now.

# CHAPTER THREE

*I* was dismissed from the palace that very day and sent back to Hatfield.

My father saw me after Mass and I had to muster all my strength not to tremble in his presence. Fortunately Cat Ashley came with me and stood to one side while I knelt at Father's feet and begged his forgiveness.

"She acted in haste and emotion," Cat Ashley said in my behalf.

"So do most women. It's their ruination. I am thinking of sending Katharine to the Tower because of just such failings. By God's teeth, I'll not have a daughter of mine behave so indiscriminately. Back to Hatfield you go to learn some common sense, child."

I thought when I heard the word *child* that there was

some warmth in his voice, some caring. I would have done anything at that moment to be forgiven.

We left soon afterward. I was in disgrace.

As I was helped into my litter by Richard Vernon, he winked at me. "You did your best, Lady Elizabeth," he whispered. "Everyone thinks so."

My father never came to see me at Hatfield that summer of 1544. And he never wrote. Nor did I write to him. Cat Ashley urged me to. So did my knights. But I felt myself wronged by him, and my stubborn temper, equal to his, would not let me go a-begging to be taken back into his affections.

Betimes, however, he did allow my brother, Edward, to visit, and Edward was now attended upon by my friend Robin. So my dear friend would be in the party, besides numerous members of Edward's household. And Robin would help me catch up with what went on at court.

"Your father has forgiven Katharine Parr for her indiscretions," he told me.

"Was she indeed a wanton?"

"No. She was worse. A radical. She was having her own thoughts about religion. Your father cannot tolerate that. But don't worry. They are back together again. Your father decided she is but a woman with all the imperfections natural to the weakness of her sex. And his mind is on other things. The invasion of France. He is readying his army. And the Act of Succession. He is going to restore you and Mary in line for the throne."

I had heard rumors of such. "So he forgives me, then?"

"Enough to have you declared, once again, Princess Elizabeth."

"But not enough to invite me back to court?"

"Why don't you write to him?"

"I can't."

"You share more than his red hair, I see. He is King, Elizabeth. Before he is your father."

"Let him decide if he wants to be a father or not."

"Then write to Katharine. She still wants to bring the family together."

As always, he helped me figure out the problem. Katharine! Of course! Word had it that since their falling out, my father had bestowed upon her the sweetest of benedictions.

"My own Robin. What would I do without you?"

"One more thing," he added. "Sir Thomas Seymour has returned from his post abroad. It is said your father knows of his feelings for Katharine. And now he's made him Lord High Admiral and sent him away again to the Kentish coast, against the French invasion."

My face flamed. Robin knew of my fascination with Sir Thomas Seymour. I tried to walk past Robin now, but he stood in my path. "Elizabeth," he said firmly. "Half the court of women are in love with Thomas Seymour. I don't care about that. I care about you and what this says of your father."

I made myself look at him. "What does it say?"

"Your father can make people he doesn't like, people who offend him, disappear, Elizabeth. In one way or another. Don't be one of those people. Write to Katharine Parr and get back in his good graces. She will help you."

For all his saying that women had weaknesses, my father made Katharine regent when he left for the invasion of France the second week in July, though he also left her with four male advisers. Katharine went to Dover with him to kiss him good-bye. I wished I could be there. Robin told me that my father had assembled the largest and most powerful force since the height of the Hundred Years' War.

It left on the night tide and arrived at Calais on the fourteenth of July. How I wished I were a boy so I could go with him! How I wished I were Queen and it was my powerful force!

I felt cheated, left out. On the twenty-fifth he lay siege to Boulogne, France's leading Channel port. On the eighteenth of September he entered Boulogne in triumph.

I knew my father enough to understand what his mood would be. And so I sat down and wrote to Katharine, congratulating her on running the kingdom in my father's absence and begging her to invoke his forgiveness of his most unworthy daughter.

Katharine had been writing to him all along. And so she made her appeal for me. My father's mood was so ebullient that he himself wrote to me, telling me of his siege and that, in celebration thereof, he was sending me a real tutor to educate me properly, in light of my new place in line for the throne.

His name was William Grindal, and he appeared at Hatfield on horseback one day with a note of recommendation in hand from a true man of letters, Roger Ascham. And so my real education began. The Latin and Greek became more difficult. And then there was the script I must learn to write, with pen and ink and swirling flourishes.

I practiced it for hours. I broke silver pen after silver pen. I spilled the ink. I cried. And the only thing that kept me at it was when Mr. Grindal told me one day, "You must practice and practice, for one day you will be signing papers as the Queen of England. It can't be an ordinary signature. It must stand out on its own."

It meant much to me, but what he said next meant more.

"Reports are sent to your father regularly. And if you bend your head to the task of your lessons, you will truly earn his respect, I promise you. I will help you get back in his favor."

Reports were sent, and I did finally get back in his favor.

One day, when William Grindal had been tutoring me for eight months, we had a visitor in the person of Jean Belmain, the French tutor of my brother, Edward. We welcomed him into the schoolroom, and he conversed with me in French for half an hour.

Apparently this dear man returned to court and told my

father that it was like conversing with a woman of forty rather than eleven, for shortly after, Cat Ashley came into my bedchamber, breathless with excitement.

"You are invited to court. You and your sister and brother. Your father wants to display you, his family, to everyone."

I felt a thrill of fear.

"Why?" I asked.

"To restore you formally to a place in the succession, after Edward."

I could not believe it. "It must have been because of what Jean Belmain told my father about me," I said.

"He didn't say anything that wasn't true, my lady. Now you must be on your best behavior this time. And we must think about a dress."

And I knew finally that my hard work with my lessons had earned me a good reputation. I was beholden to William Grindal. He had restored many silver pens for me, and now I could write beautifully in the italic hand and respond to my own invitation.

CHAPTER FOUR

*T*he gown must please my father. In his court, dress was all—so Cat Ashley kept saying while the dressmakers hovered around me, taking my measurements, remarking on how I looked the part of the Princess, and sewing far into the night.

The gown must please my father. And so it was made. Orange-red velvet stamped with the King's Tudor rose, the leaves and flowers blossoming all over and appearing again in the raised gold cutwork of the kirtle and oversleeves. There would be a girdle of pearls and rubies around my waist. Rubies trimmed the neck and sleeves. On my head I would wear a coronet as a headdress. On my feet, rose-worked velvet.

I would indeed be a Princess. If only for this night.

First there was the private audience, attended by only Katharine; my brother, Edward; and myself.

Down massive halls I went, followed by Cat and preceded by the Vernon brothers in their full knights' regalia. Armed guards snapped to attention as we passed. A knock on a massive, black, shiny door with brass handles.

"Who comes hither?"

"The Lady Elizabeth."

"Enter."

"It's about time, girl. You're late."

Had I seen a lion lying there and growling at me I would not have been surprised. My father, the lion, was slumped in his throne in the presence chamber. The smells near overpowered me. There was the sickly sweet smell of too many flowers. The room was full of them, likely meant to drown out the reek of blood and pus that came from his bandaged leg. To see it, extended in front of him, bandaged and sporting a bright spot of red blood, was a shock. And then the size of him! Why, his face was so fat that his eyes had trouble peering out at me. *This is my father,* I told myself. *This is the King. This is the man who won recently against the French. The hero.*

I near choked from the smell, then caught myself, realizing, *Why, this man is sick! This man is dying!* He had the cast of death on his face, the pallor.

Treasonous thoughts, for one never spoke or even thought of death in connection with the King. Yet still, was that why he now named his children in the proper order of succession to the throne?

Edward would be King if my father died. My brother, Edward, just seven years old.

"Stop staring, girl. Come on in. It's me. Your father."

I heard the great door slam behind me. I knew my knights and Cat Ashley were on the other side. I went forward and knelt at his feet.

Above us on the walls were murals of Diana, Actaeon, Cynthia, and Endymion hunting in green, wild woodlands. Persian carpets covered the floor. A gold-encrusted chair was brought over for me, but I mustn't rise. He must raise me up.

"Ah, you look like a Princess. Doesn't she, Kate?"

"She looks like you, love. Her red hair, her face."

He put a fat hand under my chin and raised me up. "Elizabeth," he said. "Thank heaven there is nothing of your mother in your looks. Sit, child. Tell me about your studies. Say hello to your brother."

Edward got up from his seat and came to put his arms around me. "Sister," he said, "I am so glad you have pleased our father enough to have your place restored. The Lord bless him and keep him for his kindnesses to us all."

"Hear, hear," Katharine said. She was seated at my father's other side on a velvet-topped footstool, leaning toward the King, who wore a fur-trimmed red velvet robe faced with gold-of-Venice trimming. On his head he wore his usual small cap, just a little to the side, sporting a feather.

"Some wine!" he bellowed. "We will have wine, by the gods, to celebrate the return of the Princess Elizabeth."

People scurried about. Wine and gold-encrusted goblets were brought forth and my father poured it out, one gobletful for each of us.

"To my father, the King." Edward stood up, and in a strong, pure voice gave a toast. "He who, in all his glory, sees all and determines all and never errs in his judgment."

Edward was well schooled, I thought. We all drank. The wine was too bitter for me, but I forced myself to swallow it.

Then my father spoke. "Back in thirty-two, the Friar Peto said that if I put aside Catherine of Aragon and took your mother as my wife, I should be as Ahab and the dogs would lick up my blood when I died. What did he know? That marriage broke my heart but it gave me the beautiful Elizabeth, hey?" And he tickled me under the chin.

I lowered my eyes demurely. He never spoke of my mother, they said. Some said he still loved her. I knew the reputation she had in court. She was the dark side of me, the side I must constantly fight against. Did that mean he loved me, just a bit?

"Food!" my father yelled. "Where is my tram? We must go to the banquet room!"

Immediately a chairlike, velvet-trimmed apparatus was brought forth by four yeomen of the guard, who lowered it in front of my father.

Did he no longer walk, then? He did not. There was a great to-do while the four attendants helped him into the chair and the leg was positioned. "Lead," he directed Katharine. "We sup now."

Out of the presence chamber, then, in a parade of grunts and shouts of "Clear the way, the King approaches!" we made our way down the gold-arched, mural-painted halls, past windows with red damask curtains, and swiftly, on our approach, the doors to the banquet room were opened.

"The King! All rise! The King!"

Inside a whole company of people was assembled: chancellors, bishops, members of the privy council, ladies-in-waiting, women of the court, and my father's fool, Will Somers, whose job it was to jest and make him laugh.

There was another great commotion getting my father into his chair at the head of the table. Then a signal for all to rise from their knees and sit.

The table was laden with food. Colorful salads, stewed pigeons, fresh carp in lemon sauce, partridges stewed in wine, stork in pastry, cheese in sugar, cherries in clotted cream, oysters wrapped in bacon—and the cake, oh, the cake, in the shape of Whitehall Palace!

And through all of this, my mind wondered, *Where was Mary, my sister? Was she not restored in the line of succession, too?*

Dare I ask? I dared not.

Halfway through the meal, leaning to one side and resting on Edward's arm, my father rose and made a speech.

"I do hereby declare that having taken to wife Katharine, by whom as yet there is no child, if there are yet offspring, such offspring will be placed after Prince Edward in succession to the throne. Failing any issue from my present marriage, after Edward would come Lady Mary and then the Lady Elizabeth."

Cheers and clapping. I had to rise, after Edward, and curtsey. But where was Mary?

"Your sister has fallen out of grace with me," my father said as we sat back down. "She still has Mass said in her apartments every morning. She still calls the Pope the leader of the church. When she decides that we no longer have to do with the Pope, I will welcome her back into the fold."

And I thought *I* had inherited his stubbornness. I had to admire Mary, after all, for going against him. It was true, then, what Robin had said, that my father could make people disappear if he did not approve of them. Mary had, for all intents and purposes, disappeared.

Then the music started and people, with the King's permission, got up to dance. And I saw Sir Thomas Seymour coming across the room. I hadn't known he was back. Oh, I shivered seeing him! I nibbled a sweet candied violet as I watched him. He seemed taller now, the Lord High Admiral, and more comfortable in his skin. He strode, he did not walk. And he came right to me and bowed.

"Princess, may I have this dance?"

I looked at my father, who nodded yes, then at Katharine. She was looking away and Sir Thomas did not look at her. So then, they must be in love with each other, as gossip had it. Otherwise he would have asked her, first, to dance.

I glided out across the floor with Sir Thomas as if it were the most natural thing in the world.

"This night is a new beginning for you," he said.

"Oh," I said modestly, "I'm sure being named Princess is just a formality."

"You jest, surely. From here on in you will be regarded as a desirable royal bride to be negotiated for formally."

I made a face.

"You must act accordingly, Elizabeth," he advised. "How old are you now?"

"Near eleven."

"Almost a woman. There will be many offers for your hand."

"I'll just refuse."

"Don't worry," he said. "I'll wed you first to keep you from disaster."

Oh, that he should say such. My face flamed. My heart beat faster. We kept going like that all through the dance, moving around each other verbally like fireflies. And when the dance was finally over, I was exhausted.

My father embraced me that night. He gathered me into his family circle and I could see how hard he was trying to be the father he never had been. Once, when he gestured for me to sit next to him, he leaned forward and whispered, "I've always loved you, Elizabeth. You know that, don't you?"

The question was there in the blue eyes. The pleading for forgiveness. I felt sorry for him, this mighty King, because I sensed he did not know how to love. Some people just don't, I suppose. But when I answered yes to his question I meant it. Was I so shallow then that I could forget the years of neglect? Just give me wine and good food and a title and I would melt? Did I need love so desperately?

I did. I had no mother. I thought of her that night. I knew that wherever I went I took part of her with me. I was sure my father saw that. Did he still love her somewhat? Was it possible?

I left, thinking it was. But I must not act like her, ever. She had been a flirt, a wanton, a witch. She had broken his heart. When I knelt at his feet and parted with him that night, I hoped he saw in me himself and not my mother.

## CHAPTER FIVE

*M*y life changed after that. For one thing, over the next two years, I went to court often, and the more I attended, the more self-confidence I got. I watched Edward, my brother, who surely knew that one day soon he would be King. My father's health kept failing. Edward acted like a King already. He didn't ask for things, he gave orders, and my father repeated them and laughed.

For another thing, the allowance for my clothes was finally as it should be for a King's daughter. No more did I have to watch Cat Ashley pressing her lips together as she tried to cut down one of her old gowns to make me a new one. Now yards and yards of material were delivered. Silk, velvet, brocades, satin, special sleeves, and girdles of pearls. Now Cat Ashley stood and supervised the dressmakers as they cut and fitted and basted.

And presents came to Hatfield in a constant stream. One day a box would arrive from some nobleman's wife, containing a cambric smock decorated with black silk and edged with gold spangles. Another day, another box from another nobleman, containing sleeves decorated with red roses on white silk.

From Mary came a gown of white satin with Tudor roses on the bodice and sleeves. From my father came jewelry, a necklace of opals and rubies. A ruby cross that I wore every day. The list went on and on.

From Robin came an iced cake in the shape of a castle with a circular keep and stables with candied horses. And a note: "I hope someday I may be your Master of Horse."

If anyone knew horses it was Robin. At each visit I made to court we rode out. But first I would go with him to the stables and he would pick out the horses for me and for my knights. "The roan for Princess Elizabeth," he'd order the stable boy. "She needs no spurring and will easily respond to your touch."

I had a new purple velvet riding habit and new boots that I loved to wear. And so we would ride out across the chase, at least five miles from the palace, into the woods of oak, ash, and thorn trees. Deer scampered in front of us. Rabbits and squirrels hopped out of our way. Sunlight streamed down through the branches of the trees and gave a benediction to our friendship.

And Robin would fill me in on doings at the palace since my last visit:

"Every day the doctor has to open the wound on your father's leg and let the evil out."

And: "He has made his peace with Mary. He realizes there is nothing he can do about her Catholic habits, short of sending her to the Tower. And he wants the Tudor family to be revered, so he would never do that to a child of his loins."

And: "Edward grows into more of a prig every day."

"Robin, you speak of the future King!" I tried to sound angry, to scold him as a Queen would scold. Then he tried to be penitent and we both ended up laughing.

And: "There will be no Progress this summer. Your father is too ill to travel."

I was disappointed in that. Every summer the King went on a Progress, which was a trip through his kingdom, staying at the castles and homes of his noblemen. Part of it was to see if any of the noblemen in the kingdom had enough men and arms to amass an army to rise against him. The given reason, though, was that the palaces where he lived had to be "sweetened" after the long winter. The rooms needed to be swept clean of droppings, of evil-smelling rushes. Draperies and walls were cleaned, rooms were washed from top to bottom. Rugs were beaten, beds aired, kitchens cleaned of vermin.

I had wanted, in my new royal personage, to go on a Progress, to go from royal estate to royal estate, to be wined and dined, to be entertained, to play at tennis, quoits, and archery, to ride to hounds, to go hawking.

*When I am Queen,* I decided, *I will go on a Progress every summer, if I have to be carried in a litter. I will go out and visit my people, and be entertained.*

I was thinking more and more in that vein lately, it seemed. Watching what went on about me and saying to myself: "When I am Queen . . ."

What a thrill it gave me. What a sense of power. I enjoyed it in little dribs and drabs when I saw the way people looked at me now. They were respectful. They bowed and curtseyed. They cast sidelong looks at me, likely thinking, "Watch yourself now, she may be Queen someday."

When Robin and I rode out, the people on the roads or in the fields stopped their work. The men took off their hats. The women curtseyed. "God bless you, Princess!" they shouted.

I liked it.

But there were life's lessons to learn too. And Mr. Grindal, my tutor, taught them to me along with archery that summer.

"You must learn patience, Princess. Don't be so hungry to have everything you want in a minute." Was I becoming impatient to be Queen? Did it show?

And: "Pray your father lives a while yet. The people don't like a boy-king. It means he must have a Lord Protector, and that Protector will run the kingdom. It's in the Good Book: 'Woe to the land where the King is a child.'

Right now there are two very powerful, influential families vying to be Protector. The very Catholic Howards and the New Faith Seymours. Such battles become ugly and often destroy families."

"You mean Sir Thomas Seymour?"

"More, his elder brother, the Earl of Hertford. He's a royal favorite of your father's. He's fought in many campaigns and is on the privy council, besides being brother to your Edward's mother. You must learn these things."

And: "Don't ever talk religion at court. Since your father broke with Rome and founded the New Faith, it is the most heated subject. Assure him at every turn that you acknowledge him as head of the Church. And don't ever go to Mass at the invitation of your sister, Mary."

And: "Your father's biggest heartbreak is that he didn't sire enough sons. All he ever wanted was sons. He broke from Rome so he could marry your mother in hopes of having a son. You must show him fierce determination, courage, and the ability to think clearly. You must make him glad he has you for a daughter."

I don't know what I would have done without Mr. Grindal. He taught me far more than Latin and Greek. He gave me lessons for life.

That summer of 1546 I was twelve. I would be thirteen in September. It was the most beautiful summer I remember. Not too hot and not too much rain. The crops would be lush in the fall. As a future Queen, Mr. Grindal told me, I must always have an eye cast for the crops, for if the crops failed there would be no food and the people would riot.

In the King's knot garden, the herbs, thyme, sweet hyssop, chamomile, and strawberries grew twice their normal size. The roses were perfect in shape and color, and the air was pungent with the sweet smell of fresh hay cut in the fields outside Whitehall Palace.

I did not see my father much that summer and fall. He stayed in his own apartments. Matters of state were conducted in there, though he did give a Christmas speech to Parliament, which some say had most of the members in tears.

Katharine slept on a trundle bed beside his in his room, like a servant in case he needed her. Mr. Grindal told me that my father was failing rapidly.

During the Christmas season there would be no entertainments, no feasts, no masques, no dancing. The court was closed to all but members of the privy council. Mr. Grindal told me that my father was readying matters of state for his death, making provisions for people, drawing up his will.

I went home to Hatfield for Christmas. Edward came home with me, as if in a last act that would be played out as brother and sister before he became King. We decorated Hatfield with berries and greens. We had a Yule log. My servants prepared a Christmas feast: half a dozen pike in calf's-foot jelly, capon breasts in golden cream, plates of filberts, pheasant in wine sauce, quinces, marchpane, wafers, and cordials for the adults. Mr. Grindal, Cat Ashley, and my knights dined with us.

I finished working on a white satin doublet I was making for my brother as a gift.

They say that when my father died, they did not announce it to the world for three days. Only Katharine—now to be the Queen Dowager—was told.

I was abed at Hatfield when I heard the galloping horses in my sleep. They galloped right through the darkness of my dreams, ripping apart the black curtain between them and reality. I sat up.

"Princess."

It was Cat, at the door, holding a candle.

"Your presence is required. Downstairs."

As I stumbled into the cold corridor I saw Edward coming down the hall, surrounded by his knights. They nodded at us and we proceeded down the winding stairway, every step a torture to my soul.

The scene was a dream now: servants holding candles, dark figures in the background, a hooded man just inside the threshold surrounded by soldiers.

What were these strange soldiers doing in my house in the middle of the night?

The man nodded at me and then at Edward. Then he slipped off his hood.

It was Edward Seymour, the Lord of Hertford.

Immediately he knelt before us. "The King is dead. Long live the King," he said, addressing Edward. "Sire, God has called your father to eternal rest. You are the King, our lord and governor. Please you accept my life as yours, my service to command."

I glanced at Edward. He looked pale and childlike one moment, and in the next he drew himself up and it was as if someone had put a piece of armor on his shoulders.

He replied something, I don't know what; the roaring in my ears was so loud. But I am sure he had practiced it many times.

Then I caught Mr. Grindal's eye. He nodded and lowered his eyes, knelt. All of them did and I too fell on my knees. I stayed that way until Lord Hertford and Edward went into an inner chamber.

Sometime in the small hours of the morning, when the sky was gray satin and there were no stars, I heard them leaving. I got out of bed, put on my robe, and went out into the hallway. Over the balustrade I saw them: Lord Hertford, all his soldiers and attendants, and my brother, Edward.

Before he went out the great arched front door into the cold, Edward turned and looked up at me. He raised his arm in farewell. I think there were tears in his eyes.

I heard Mr. Grindal's words in my head: "It's in the Good Book. 'Woe to the land where the King is a child.'"

It had something to do with etiquette, Mr. Grindal told me. Women did not attend the funerals of Kings.

My father had given directions. He wanted to be buried in the vault next to Jane Seymour, Edward's mother. So his body was carried on a chariot covered with cloth of gold to the chapel of Syon Abbey. There, overnight, the lead coffin burst open because of his weight. And blood seeped onto the church floor.

The next morning men came to repair the coffin. With them was a dog. A black dog who licked up the blood from the floor. Most people knew of the prophecy of Friar Peto by now, and those present were near to terror.

The coffin was then carried into St. George's Chapel, Windsor, where my father was laid to rest next to Jane Seymour.

Then all those officers who had served in his household broke their staves over their heads and threw them into the vault, signifying that they would serve no one else.

*"Le roi est mort!"* the black-clad mourners shouted. *"Vive le roi!"*

The King is dead. Long live the King.


I was ordered by the privy council to go back to the palace and keep Queen Katharine company, one of the good things to come out of my father's death.

My father left Mary and me money. I don't know what Mary received in his will, but I was allotted three thousand pounds a year and a marriage portion of ten thousand pounds. There were also manors, jewels, and the increased devotion of my underlings, who saw me now as a serious contender for the throne, should my brother die without issue.

As Mr. Grindal had suggested, Edward Seymour was named by Father as my brother's Protector. To assuage the jealousy of his brother, Sir Thomas, Edward Seymour gave Sir Thomas the titles Baron Seymour of Sudeley Castle and Lord High Admiral for life.

"He must be really strutting around now, that attractive man. You do find him attractive, don't you, Elizabeth?" Cat asked me one day.

"Of course."

"He is attracted to you," she said knowingly.

I had long since learned to listen to Cat. She had a grapevine of information that could wind all the way around Hatfield, and as with most ladies-in-waiting, her information was usually correct.

"How do you know? He's near forty. I'm not yet fourteen."

"Oh, he's been attracted for years. Everyone knows that. What would you do if he came courting?"

"He would have to ask permission of my little brother, Edward."

She smiled knowingly. "Know your own mind, Elizabeth" was all she would say. "You are the one who has to be wife to someone someday."

"I don't think I will wed," I countered.

"You must. Especially if you are to be Queen."

"Hush. You mustn't bandy such words about, Cat. You could get into trouble. In any case, Mary would be Queen before me."

She scowled. "Edward is not that well. Always was sickly. Mary is thirty-one already and never has been healthy. Be careful, Elizabeth. If Sir Thomas approaches, be careful."

I waved off her warnings and predictions. Then I had a thought. Was Sir Thomas attracted to me because I might someday truly be Queen? Then why not first approach Mary? But I had the answer. Mary was Catholic. He could not bring himself to align himself with her, Queen or not. I went back to my embroidery, thinking that things were moving too fast. I wanted, above all, to see my brother, the King. But Edward Seymour refused to allow him to see his half sisters or even Dowager Queen Katharine. He wanted my brother to be influenced by him and no one else.

How did Edward fare? Neither Mary nor I had been invited to his coronation, which had been held on a damp-to-the-bones day in February. Archbishop Cranmer administered the coronation oath. I was told Edward looked small and lost under his new crown. And I wondered what Edward was thinking when Cranmer told my brother he was God's anointed and supreme head of the Church.

Within weeks of my father's death, Cat Ashley placed an important-looking letter in my hand.

It was from Sir Thomas Seymour.

He asked, in no uncertain terms, for my hand in marriage.

I flushed, at first with pleasure. Then pride. I was not yet fourteen but I was something he desired, someone picked out of all the women at court for this high honor. My head swam as I pondered what marriage to this handsome, popular, and accomplished man would be like.

Then something stopped me. The privy council would likely say no, and their blessing, as well as Edward's, was necessary for such a wedding to take place. I was no longer the Lady Elizabeth, after all. I was Princess Elizabeth, third in line for the throne. I must marry royalty.

Everyone knew that Sir Thomas Seymour was an ambitious man.

I must show people I was capable of making important decisions on my own. That I was not some starstruck little girl. So I took up my silver pen, and on the best parchment I could find and in my best script, I wrote a letter to Sir Thomas, declining his offer.

"Neither my age nor my inclination allows me to think of marriage," I told him. "I need at least two years of mourning for my father before contemplating such a move."

I sent the letter by special courier, but I never recovered from the pride his offer gave me.

It was decided by the council that I should live with my stepmother because I was too young to live alone.

In March I moved, with my household and knights, to the old manor house at Chelsea, a place my father had built in 1536. Katharine was already living there. The place reminded me of St. James's Palace, as it was made of rosy brick and built around two quadrangles. It had three halls, three parlors, three kitchens, three drawing rooms, seventeen chambers, and casement windows, and its water was brought in from Kensington by conduit. It was but an hour's ride from court. I had spent a summer there with my cousin Catherine Howard when she was my father's Queen, and I remembered it as a pleasant place, more manor house than palace. In the summer, damask roses bloomed all the way down to the river. The grounds had cherry, peach, and nut trees, five acres of gardens in all. But it was winter now as we approached the place, and the river was full of ice floes.

A whole complement of attendants came out to welcome us, to help us from our horses, to gather our baggage, to guide us to the great entranceway inside, where candles glowed and a fire burned in the great hearth in the center hall.

"Princess Elizabeth, welcome to your new home."

Katharine and I hugged and as she drew me into her arms I felt the familiar fragrance of her, my father's wife, my stepmother, and now my hostess. I looked around. The house was beautifully appointed and I saw her touch everywhere, in the profusion of bright tapers on the walls, the deep carpets, the tapestries with scenes of the Old Testament, the boxes of sweetmeats, the applewood fire burning in the hearth.

*I think I will like it here,* I told myself. Little did I know that it would be the stage for the most sordid period of my life.

Katharine had a welcoming dinner for me that night, and it was almost as elaborate as the ones I'd attended at court. I wondered how she dared, when she was supposed to be in mourning.

Then I noticed. Though Katharine wore mourning clothes, she did not seem to be in mourning. The black velvet gown was low cut and showed her bosoms. The bright jewels bespoke no sadness. There was a special light in her eyes, a special color to her cheeks as she went about speaking to everyone. Her guests were many and her household was very large, as befitted a Queen, with many ladies-in-waiting, of whom I was to be the chief one.

As I walked through the crowd greeting everyone, I came upon two girls a bit younger than I. "Hello, Lady Elizabeth," the older one said with a curtsey.

At first I did not recognize her. It was my cousin Lady Jane, the one I disliked for her religious fervor and her parrot's tongue. The girl never had an original thought in her head but was quoting the Bible all the time.

"The proper title these days is Princess Elizabeth," I said tartly.

The other girl was her little sister, Catherine. They clung together like orphans in a storm. For all I had heard about her, Jane might as well have been an orphan. Her parents sometimes beat her. She could never please them no matter what she did. Being so scholarly, she would never make a good marriage, they constantly complained. And they had grandiose plans for her.

I hoped I wasn't supposed to be a friend to them. I hoped they were not invited to stay as I was. Lady Jane was short, with a pallid face full of freckles. Nature seemed to have denied her color. Her hair was washed-out-looking in comparison with mine. Her voice was hesitant, her manner humble.

I was polite to her and her sister that night, but I was glad that they went home the next day. Lady Jane annoyed me, if only because I knew I might be like her if I didn't fight against my fears and my lack of courage every day.

When she parted from Katharine, Lady Jane smiled up at her. "So Sir Thomas will come soon to ask my parents?" she asked.

"As soon as we are settled and he can," Katharine promised.

What was this? Sir Thomas Seymour? Come where? To Lady Jane's house?

And what did she mean, "As soon as we are settled?"

After they departed I looked at Katharine, but before I got the chance to ask, she reached out her hand to me. "Come inside. I must talk with you," she said.

"Elizabeth, we have much to discuss."

We were seated in her bedchamber. An applewood fire burned in the hearth. Yeomen of the guard stood at attention outside her door. Her bedchamber was more than for bed. She would sometimes, I was to learn, receive visitors in here, sometimes entertain her closest friends. Rich tapestries sealed off the bed. Sweetmeats were offered, and I sensed that something important was coming. I was, for the moment, frightened. As far as I knew, she did not know of Sir Thomas Seymour's proposal to me, and I vowed to keep it secret. But I was afraid now that she had found out and was offended.

"I admire your intelligence so, your education. But I think it is time for you to have a new tutor. I think you have learned all there is to learn from Mr. Grindal."

I tried not to show my relief. "Yes," I said.

"Elizabeth, there is a man who was Grindal's teacher. His name is Roger Ascham. He is a humanist scholar of Latin and Greek classics, and was appointed to be a Reader in Greek at St. John's College, Cambridge. He has written a book, has a passion for archery, and for a while tutored your brother, Edward. What say you?"

I said yes. Mr. Grindal, she said, would not be hurt. He had the urge to travel.

But there was more.

"The Lady Jane is going to come and live with us. Sir Thomas has paid her father, bought himself her guardianship. He has a great interest in the girl, who has had an unfortunate home life. I wish you to be a friend to her."

I said nothing.

"Elizabeth, keep in mind that you may someday be Queen," she said softly. "Everything we do, Sir Thomas and

I, is with that possibility in mind."

And then she said something else. "I promised my husband I would speak to you about it. He has great expectations of you."

From outside came the barking of dogs. Downstairs a door slammed. I heard someone drop some dishes in the kitchen.

Husband? My father was dead scarce two months. I am afraid that my mouth fell open. "Who?" my voice cracked, but I already knew. I already felt the knell of doom.

"That is the other favor. That you keep my secret. I'm planning on getting married. To Sir Thomas Seymour. He has asked for my hand, and you know he was an old love of mine."

Know? Certainly she was jesting. "Yes," I said. "The grand courtier. All women, children, and dogs are in love with him. When are you planning on doing this?"

"As soon as possible. But I haven't asked Edward's permission."

"Edward. My little brother?"

"The King," Catherine said. "Don't forget he's the King."

"You would marry in secret, then?"

"Yes. Do you think Edward will be very angry when he finds out?"

"I know Edward loves you."

"You know Sir Thomas and I were near to plighting our troth before your father asked me to wed him. We have been in love for a long time. I have wed three times when I was not in love, because it was my duty to do so. Now I want to wed for myself. For me."

"I know Edward loves his uncle Tom too," I said. "Sir Thomas always treated him more like a man, not like a child the way his brother, the Protector, does."

"Will you keep my secret, then? I plan to go away for a week after we wed."

"Yes."

"I'm telling everyone I'm going to stay with my sister. Do you promise?"

"I promise," I said. "But I thought . . . that I was to be the only one here. I mean, to enjoy the hospitality of your house."

"You will still be the most important. Thomas is very impressed with you. We want to say we had a part in your upbringing. Come now, don't pout. Thomas doesn't like ladies who pout."

## CHAPTER SIX

"What do you mean, you're leaving?"

He stood before me, Robin did, in all his new height, more like a seventeen-year-old than his thirteen years, his head bowed. "We're leaving court, my father and brothers and I."

"Why?"

"My father had a fight with Gardiner, the Lord Bishop of Winchester. They came to blows. My father hit Gardiner in the face."

"Robin, one doesn't do that in court."

He drew himself up proudly. "My father had just cause."

"What was the fight about?"

"A matter in the privy council. The division of power. It is tipping."

"In whose favor?"

He didn't say. "They await me, my father and brothers. I must leave." He came and knelt on one knee at my feet. "My childhood friend, I don't know when I will see you again."

I raised him up and we stood but a foot apart. His face already showed the hint of a beard. Already it was molded in the lines of a man. I felt a pang of fear. Was I losing everybody? First Sir Thomas because of his marriage to Katharine, and now my dear friend Robin?

"God go with you," I said.

He nodded and kissed my forehead. "Be careful, Elizabeth. There is danger all around."

"I'll be safe here."

He shook his head no, ever so slightly. "All around," he said. He had taken my hand in his and now he turned to go, reluctantly dropping my fingers. His sword clattered, his boots sounded as he left the room.

I had not told him of Sir Thomas's marriage proposal, but somehow I had the feeling that he knew all about it. And more.

My sister, Mary, had spies. She had to. As someone who was next in line for the throne, she had to know whom she could and could not trust. I knew she had spies in court, and likely even in the privy council.

Now she wrote to me from Wanstead, one of her estates, asking me to come and live with her, telling me I was more than welcome and saying that since Katharine was marrying the Lord High Admiral, things must be uncomfortable for me at Chelsea.

So she knew about the wedding, just as it was about to happen. She knew about my former attraction to Sir Thomas. What else did she know? Something told me I must be kind, yet wary, toward this sister who was seventeen years older than I. Someday she would be Queen, a devout Catholic Queen, determined to bring England back to Rome.

As a member of the new Reformed Faith who despised everything Catholic, where did that put me?

Katharine left to wed Sir Thomas. She left with a bevy of her ladies and yeomen of the guard for London, where the wedding would take place at the home of her half sister and brother-in-law, Lady and Lord Herbert.

They returned in two weeks. Sir Thomas had with him a whole complement of men on horseback, including knights and guards. He had extra horses, dogs, and even his hawks. The big house became alive the way it does when a man is about, alive with laughter, back-slapping, joking, wagering— even cursing—boots scraping, servants bowing and attending, and dogs everywhere, wagging their tails and settling at their masters' feet.

I heard it all from upstairs in my chamber. I had a sick headache, something I'd been suffering from lately. I was fourteen now and subject to womanly ailments. I even had a fever, which gave Katharine a start and caused her to fuss over me in a way that made me feel as if I were loved.

I was sorry for myself. After all, I was an orphan, with neither mother nor father. I was going to be living under the same roof now as the man I'd always been attracted to, growing up. And he was married to the only woman who had ever really fulfilled the role of mother for me. I could be Queen someday, yet I couldn't even have a meeting with the brother I loved. And I was afraid of my only sister.

Katharine gave me a remedy for my headache and Cat Ashley brought up some soup and muffins for me. I ate hungrily. Then Katharine left to attend to the men downstairs with her husband. Cat Ashley helped me change into a frilly nightgown and brushed my long red hair. "You're going to have a visitor," she said.

"Who?"

I never dreamed it would be he. But it was. In the next minute he was there, standing in my chamber in all his maleness, bringing in the scent of horse and outside, of health and vigor.

"Well, we meet again, Princess."

"My Lord." I nodded my head, and my eyes went over him, his leather jerkin, the ruff at his neck, the soft velvet of his jacket, his high black boots, his sword, his hat with the feather in it. And I thought, *He should have been mine. Devoted only to me. Like Robin and Cat Ashley.*

He came to the bed, bowed, took my hand and kissed it. He sat down on the edge of the bed. "I am your stepfather now," he said, as if that excused the familiarity. "Cat tells me you haven't been eating."

"I ate this night."

"Well, I bid you get well. There is a favor we need from you."

"And what could I possibly do for a Dowager Queen and a Lord High Admiral?"

"We didn't get permission from the King for our marriage. Or from the privy council. The council will be livid, as will my brother. If your brother forgives us and gives the marriage his blessing, all will be well. Would you like to visit Edward and clear the way for us? He'll do it if you ask."

*Well,* I thought, *he did ask me to wed him first.* Had I said yes, he wouldn't be wed to Katharine now.

"I would love to see Edward," I said. "When can I go?"

He smiled and took my hand. "Get well first, and then as soon as possible," he said.

Katharine had left Whitehall Palace without her Queen's jewels. So she wrote, asking Sir Thomas's brother, the Lord Protector, for them. A letter came to her with great dispatch. The Lord Protector was so angry that they had married without his permission that he refused to send the jewels. "Suppose you are with child?" he asked her. "How are we to determine if it is the late King's or not? You are destined for a more profitable match on the world stage," he wrote. "My brother had no right to steal you away."

No. The jewels would stay where they were, in the Treasury, until such time as the King married. Then they would go to his wife.

Katharine was furious and refused to go to court all spring, especially, she said, because she knew the Lord Protector's wife would be prancing around in the jewels.

To assuage his brother's anger at Katharine's being refused the jewels, the Lord Protector gave Castle Sudeley to Sir Thomas, which dated from the fifteenth century. Sir Thomas was delighted. It was just south of the village of Winch-combe, in Gloucestershire, in a beautiful park.

He ordered it refurbished. And there was peace in our house again. Though Katharine still wanted those jewels, which had been left to her by the King.

That spring it was cold and rainy and sometimes the rain turned to snow. It was no time to travel. The roads were not to be borne. Then I got a cold and had to stay abed, so it was late spring before finally I got to see my brother, Edward.

I traveled to London with my ladies-in-waiting and knights. I had heard how Edward embraced the New Faith more and more every day, how he decried the waste and spending in the court, so I discarded all my frippery and had a plain gray velvet dress made, so modest and simple that I thought it near elegant.

"You're doing the wrong thing," Cat Ashley told me. She was near tears. "You are so beautiful. You should wear your best."

But I had a favor to ask of Edward. And if I ever intended to obtain his blessing for the marriage of Sir

Thomas and Katharine, and assuage his anger at not having his permission asked, I must present myself as humble and plain, and not show myself to be just another flamboyant woman.

I wore no bejeweled headdress. I had my hair done simply, parted in the middle and allowed to hang down my back. The dress had a modest neckline. I wore no neck jewelry, no rings on my fingers. There were no earrings, no rope of pearls around my waist, and I wore no scent to attract a man.

In court I was greeted with gasps and sighs. "Make way for the Princess Elizabeth" was the cry, and all eyes turned, wide, surprised at my plainness.

Never had I seen women so dazzling in frippery, in finery. Their hair was worn in curls piled high on their heads and interwoven with pearls. Their white ruffs were like snow, gossamer thin and standing up on their necks. Their gowns were the colors of the rainbow, brocaded, with slashed sleeves that showed the finest of silks and velvets.

I approached the throne, which was under a red velvet canopy tied back with gold ropes. To reach it I had to pass through rows of armed men.

"Make way, make way, for the King's most honored sister!"

Everyone parted ranks. At the foot of the throne I knelt, as I would before my father.

"Approach. I give you leave," I heard Edward's voice, no longer high and thin but firm and manly.

I raised my eyes. Near the throne was a huge arched window overlooking the Thames River. On the river were sailboats.

Edward's little dogs were at his feet. On a nearby desk I saw a telescope and papers, charting . . . what? The tides? The movement of ships? He looked so lonely and forlorn in his robes of state.

"The Princess Elizabeth," they announced me.

Edward rose to raise me up. He hugged me. I was surprised to notice that he was taller than I now. His state robes were red and trimmed with white ermine, and under them he wore a plain gray silk suit, black hose, and shoes.

At once I noted how thin he was, how pale. How his eyes were sunken in his head.

We embraced. I wiped tears from my eyes at the sight of my little brother surrounded by guards and men of his chamber. Now he looked at them all and waved a disdainful hand. "I would be alone with my sister, the Princess. Leave me. All of you."

Reluctantly they left and there was no one left in the throne room. We were alone.

He bade me sit beside him and showed me the journal he was keeping, and his charts. I was right: The charts kept track of ships that passed his window on the Thames. "London looks so busy," I told him. "There is so much building going on."

"Yes. For one, the Lord Protector is building himself a new manor house. It must be worthy of his position, he says. He pulled down the north side of St. Paul's to do it. Men are so greedy, Elizabeth."

I noticed he was coughing.

"How goes it with you, Edward?" I asked.

"I'm fair to middling."

"Do you like being King?"

"No. I can't do anything I want. The Lord Protector won't let me see the people I want. They don't let me play at sports as much as I would like. I'm never alone for more than fifteen minutes, but I tell you, Elizabeth, there are things I will accomplish as King before I die."

I shivered. "Don't talk of dying."

"No." And he laughed. "I hear they have two men in the pillory in London for saying I am sick to the point of dying. But, Elizabeth, I have been traveling through London, and you would not believe the situation of the poor! Why, some of them have no place to live." He leaned forward toward me. He took my hand. "It is my plan to give the Palace of Bridewell to the Corporation of London to use as a workhouse for the poor. I know our father closed all the monasteries and many were taken by the noblemen, but I would give Greyfriars Monastery to be a school for poor scholars. I would have St. Thomas's Hospital used for the poor who are sick."

"God bless you, Edward," I told him.

He nodded. "I like the way you are dressed. You make fools of all the ladies of the court. Let them take example from you."

I glowed under the praise.

"Now, the matter about which you have come to see me," he said. And he picked up some folded parchment from his desk. "This is for Katharine. I write to her that she need fear no more recriminations because of her marriage. I will not tolerate them from anybody.

"After all," he told me, "she is my beloved stepmother and he my favorite uncle."

We visited a while longer. We spoke some Latin to each other. We recounted childhood memories. He asked me how I like Roger Ascham, my new tutor, and I told him I scarce knew the man yet.

"I give her my full support," he said of Katharine, "though there is nothing I can do to give her back her jewels." He sounded somewhat bitter and his face took on the angles of one far older, who knew things I did not.

I fished a gold velvet purse out of one of the pockets of my gown. "Sir Tom sends you this," I told him.

He scowled. "So then, people know that the Lord Protector won't allow me much money." He shook the purse and grinned. Then he opened it. Inside were more than enough crowns and shillings to make a nine-year-old boy happy.

"But I don't want Uncle Tom to think he's bought me off," he said.

"He knows better," I told him.

"Will you play a game of chess with me, Elizabeth?"

"Of course."

"Then, if they come in and ask you to leave, I can tell them no. Not until we are finished."


Roger Ascham was a man not of great stature but of a great mind. His eagerness showed in his face, his smile. He looked like one of those men who had not been a handsome little boy but had grown into a handsome man. His ears were a little too large, but one could not help liking him immediately.

At thirty-three he was already a foremost Greek scholar. But he was also a musician and sportsman. He had gentle brown eyes and praised my writing and my penmanship. He would teach me music and dancing, as well as Greek and Latin, mathematics and philosophy, and all the rest of the subjects a future Queen must have.

He was educating me to be Queen then. But he was not beholden to me. I liked the fact that he did not scrape and bow.

He taught me to shoot with the longbow, the same as my father had taught my mother. He told me about life at Cambridge, of dicing parties and cockfighting parties and how he had lost so much money in foolish bets.

We worked at Greek in the mornings and Latin in the afternoons. On alternate days we worked on music and dancing, philosophy, mythology, the sciences, religion.

Sometimes I caught him gazing at me across the study table when he thought I wasn't paying mind. Sometimes I thought he was looking at me more as a man would than a teacher. But I kept my distance and he respected me. And his admiration lifted my spirits. I was just beginning to learn, after all, how to behave around men.

Jane Grey moved in.

She came with a carriage full of belongings, a pet cat, books enough to stock a library, and her own tutor, Mr. Alymer. She came with tapestries of the Bible for her room, foot carpets, a bear hide for her cat to sleep on, and a bed-cover of crimson velvet. She came carrying her own pillow, like a child. And if all these possessions should seem not in the spirit of the plainness of her wardrobe and beliefs, then it was left to the onlooker to figure it out.

Her parents, after all, were rich. She must have favorite possessions.

I did not help her get settled. I must think of my position. Katharine spent the whole day supervising Jane's welcoming into her suite of rooms. She had three bed-chambers: one for herself, one for her tutor, and one for her ladies-in-waiting.

Sir Thomas gave her a welcoming gift of a doll.

Jane accepted it with grace, though I could tell by watching her that her days of playing with dolls were long past.

Sir Tom came into my room again the day after Jane arrived.

I was just lying there, enjoying the thin morning sunshine and listening to sounds from belowstairs, when the knob of my door turned and he walked in.

"I wanted to thank you for interceding with Edward for us," he said, seating himself on the foot of my bed. "It means much to both of us."

"He's my brother." I said it rather tartly. I did not like his just barging in and sitting himself down on my bed like that. After all, I was the future Queen of England, wasn't I? I was relieved when he left.

It occurred to me too that he could have thanked me at breakfast. Or at any time during the day. I did not know what to do about it, but fortunately, Cat Ashley did.

We decided to lock my door at night, though Katharine didn't like it. Suppose I needed someone during the night, she said. I pointed out that Cat Ashley slept in an anteroom and could protect me.

So for a while there were no early-morning confrontations with Sir Tom. I still secretly admired him, of course, but had not yet forgiven him for marrying Katharine just like that. As if my refusal had meant nothing to him.

And I still did not quite trust him for not telling Katharine about his proposal to me. *What kind of a man is he?* I asked myself.

I was soon to find out.

In early March of the new year, 1548, Katharine announced to everyone that she was to have a child. Finally. After three previous husbands and twenty years of marriage. She was so happy that the rest of us were happy too. Especially Sir Tom, who promptly announced that it was going to be a boy.

But just in case, he went to see an astrologer, who promised him that it would be a boy. And Sir Tom went about all puffed up, like a rooster.

And like a rooster, the first awake in the household, he started coming into my room again mornings.

He'd had, I soon discovered, his own key made for my locked door.

"It is my house," he told me when I questioned him. "There is nowhere in it I should not be allowed to go."

On one morning visit he told me he wanted me to share my tutor and my study time with Lady Jane. "Her tutor is going to Germany for a while. He will be back by summer. But we can't leave her without one. That way you will get to know her better," he said. "It seems so silly, two girls of near the same age living in separate households."

"Must I?" I said. "I have no love for her. She's a pious little parrot with her nose in a prayer book all the time."

"That's not like you, Elizabeth. That isn't the way you've been raised. You would welcome Edward studying with you."

"How do you know how I've been raised? When I was a child nobody shared anything with me. I didn't even have proper clothing. Cat Ashley had to beg my father for fabric and he never sent it."

"You're not a child any longer." His eyes went over my pink nightdress and of a sudden I wanted to pull the neckline up closer.

"Well, then, I'll decide if I want to share my tutor with Lady Jane."

"Let me know." He got up from the bed. "But you should know that you will disappoint Katharine if you appear selfish in this. And now is not the time to displease Katharine. Do you agree?"

I did not answer. He left the room.

We were seated in Katharine's apartment taking a repast at nine that night. I looked across the firelit room at Jane. She looked younger than twelve. Her hair, a mousy brown, was tucked under a head kerchief. A small nosegay of jasmine was tucked into her bodice. She wore gray, as she always did, long sleeves trimmed with ermine.

It wasn't as if she didn't have brighter clothing. My sister had sent her a dress of cloth of gold and a pearl necklace.

"When I have the baby and we celebrate, you should wear the dress Mary sent you," Katharine suggested.

Jane shook her head. "No, my lady. I suppose I shall have to wear it someday when I am Queen, but not now."

We were doing embroidery and talking. I pricked my finger with the needle. "When you are Queen?" I could scarce get the words out.

I saw her and Katharine exchange glances. Then Katharine smiled but looked down at her embroidery. "We should have told you, Elizabeth. Sir Thomas has adopted Lady Jane, with the promise to her father that he will wed her to King Edward someday soon."

My head spun. Marry this little . . . oh, I could not think of the word . . . this little mouse to my brother?

She would indeed then be Queen.

"It is not my idea," Lady Jane said modestly. "And I certainly don't want to be Queen. But if Sir Tom and His Majesty so desire, well, then, I shall do their bidding, of course."

She didn't want to be Queen, but she would do their bidding? How did things like this happen? All the while I'd been supposing and pretending and planning to be Queen, and then this little child suddenly finds herself wanted for the position?

Didn't she know that fierce battles had been fought, that thousands of men had died, that men schemed for years to take the throne? And she would take it at someone's bidding?

I wanted to force back the tears that came into my eyes. This was why I really disliked her, I thought. There was more behind those shy brown eyes than one could imagine.

She made me so angry that I wanted to slap her. "You don't know your place," I told her. "I'm third in line for the succession. You shouldn't go around talking so casually about being Queen. It's . . . Why, it's dangerous."

"Elizabeth!" Katharine gasped.

Jane started to cry. And we were like that when Sir Tom came into the room. When Katharine told him what had transpired, he looked at me sternly. "Apologize to Jane," he said.

"No. I won't. I'm the one who's going to be Queen someday. Not her. I won't apologize to anybody."

I wouldn't, either. Sir Tom sat down and took the weeping Jane onto his lap and dried her tears. Yes, I wanted to slap her, the way she leaned against him and played the helpless waif.

The next morning he came into my bedroom again.

## CHAPTER SEVEN

*H*e came in and stood there, tall and striking in his leather doublet, ruffled shirt, fancy hose, and boots.

"Still sleeping, you lazy girl?" he asked. "Come on, get up, we have things to talk about."

"Go away." I turned from him.

Then he did something that shocked me. He put his hands on me, on my shoulders, on my chemise and turned me back to him. "I want to know if you're going to study with Lady Jane."

"Take your hands off me."

But he laughed, like my old Lord Tom did when I was a child and he dispensed sweetmeats to the children in court. And then he drew the coverlet back to tickle my ribs.

"Oh, oh stop," I begged.

"Will you apologize to Lady Jane? And let her study with you?"

He wouldn't stop. And I couldn't get away. Finally I said I'd let her study with me, but I wouldn't apologize. I don't know what would have happened then if Cat Ashley hadn't come running into the room, along with two of my maids.

"What is this? What's going on here?" Cat stood, horrified, as I squirmed under Lord Tom's hands.

"Get out of here, you old witch," he told her. "I'm having a discussion with my stepdaughter. She's been disobedient and disrespectful and I must attend to it."

"Oh, Sir Tom, please. I'm responsible for the Princess. What will people say?"

"What people?" He continued to tickle me. Then he slapped me on the rump and I screamed. "What people?" he asked again.

She pointed to the maids.

"Out, out!" he ordered them, and when they just stood there staring, he shook them both and slapped them. They left, shrieking.

"They'll tell," Cat Ashley said. "It will be all over that you were in here like this."

"Not unless you tell them to, you old bag of bones." But he stopped then and looked at me.

"I'll be back tomorrow morning. And every morning until you apologize to Lady Jane," he said to me. And then he left.

But I wouldn't apologize. And I don't know why. Except that I had to admit to myself that I liked it when he came in every morning and we romped in my chamber, with the maids screaming and Cat Ashley scolding. It was exciting, and the attention he paid me was gratifying.

Someone must have told Katharine. Because she started coming in with him mornings and all three of us made a game of it.

I don't know why Katharine came with him, but I had the feeling it was because she wanted to make it a respectable game and not so scandalous. Because it *was* scandalous. It aroused in me feelings I never knew I had for him, and I began to look forward to his coming every morning. Sometimes, when only Cat Ashley was there in the room with us, she would scold him as he came at me in my bed, as his hands reached out and fumbled for me, as I lay there breathless and dazed.

"Sir, I cannot allow such goings-on with the Princess. You will soil her honor!"

"What?" And he'd lash out at her. "Fie upon you, you dirty-minded old lady. I simply call upon her because she is almost my daughter now. Fie upon your bold tongue!"

Lady Jane caught wind of it and took it upon herself to deride me. "It's a dangerous game," she told me.

"But it's only a game," I reminded her, and then: "You're simply jealous because he doesn't come into your chamber. Anyway I can't keep him out."

"You have knights. Station them outside your door," she advised.

"It's Sir Tom's house," I reminded her.

"You're asking for trouble, Elizabeth. People talk. This could be construed as treason on his part. You're in line for the throne. You can't have a married man taking over in your chamber. Please listen to me."

But I wouldn't, and so it went on, as did the summer, with Katharine's pregnant belly getting bigger and bigger and Sir Tom sometimes going into London and bringing home presents to me and to Lady Jane, who behaved as decorously as ever.

Mr. Grindal returned, and with him came the summer.

There is some malady that comes to us in the summer, like a serpent. It has always been called the sweating sickness. It came to London, it came to our house, and many of the servants caught it. I did not; nor did Katharine or Sir Tom or Lady Jane, but Mr. Grindal did.

One morning Sir Tom came upon me in the garden, where I was picking the first of the roses. "A word with you, Elizabeth," he said.

He was somber, solemn near to the point of being stern. I set down my basket of roses on a nearby bench and turned to him. He sat down on the bench near the basket.

"Mr. Grindal died last night of the sweating sickness."

I burst into tears and dropped my cutting shears on the ground. My shoulders shook with sobs. Not only for Mr.

Grindal but for my life here, for what I'd been going through, for my confusion about Sir Tom, for Katharine, for all of us.

In a moment Sir Tom had me on his lap, at first to comfort me, and then it became something else as I hugged him close and felt the maleness of him and lost myself in his arms. Soon he was kissing me, and not like an uncle or a guardian, but like a man.

"I only married Katharine so I could be close to you," he was telling me between kisses, and we were like that, pursuing each other hungrily, when there came the sound of footsteps down the walk and we both looked up to see Katharine standing there, horrified.

"Oh, oh my sweet Jesus," she said. And she grabbed the side of an arbor and sank down on the brick walk. Immediately Cat and Mr. Parry and some of Katharine's maids came to help her up.

Sir Tom pushed me off his lap, stood up, and went to kneel in front of his wife. "Sweet wife, thank God you've come to save me from this girl. She is rashly wanton. I came out to comfort her for Mr. Grindal's death and she threw herself at me. Oh, thank the Lord you are here."

Katharine said nothing. She just got to her feet, turned, and trotted clumsily back to the house.

# CHAPTER EIGHT

*I* had to admire Katharine. I don't think I could be as much the grand lady as she was if some little chit of a girl like me was caught kissing my husband.

At dinner there was no discussion of it. We sat at table, all of us, including Lady Jane, without so much as a word of rancor or blame. We discussed the approaching fall season in London and the coming of Katharine and Sir Tom's child. He had been to two astrologers, who both told him it would be a boy.

Already the first of many gifts for the nursery were coming in. A goodly shipment had come this day and Sir Tom had had them opened.

Now he recited them: "A set of silver pots and goblets. A silver porringer. Three more quilts and sets of sheets. Two pewter jugs, fashioned like animals to hold milk. A tester of scarlet. Six wall hangings."

"We must make ready the nursery soon," Katharine said.

And so went the longest meal of my life. After dinner Katharine summoned me to her private chambers.

She was sitting on a red velvet lounge chair. I knelt at her feet. She did not ask me to rise.

"My husband swears on his mother that there was no more between you than I saw," she told me. "But I fear your young blood. Don't forget, you have the blood of Anne Boleyn in your veins. You cannot help yourself, so it is my job to help you."

I lowered my eyes at this mention of my mother. The blood of Anne Boleyn, I supposed, would haunt me all of my born days.

"I know how attractive he is to a woman. Oh yes, I know. But he is my husband and I know too that he loves me. So I am sending you away. To Cheshunt, deep in the woodland valley, where you will have a chance to think and to grow. You may take Cat Ashley and Roger Ascham. I will deny you nothing. But you have not only flirted here with my husband, you have put him in danger of being accused of treason for dallying with you."

Treason! It meant losing one's head. Like my mother.

"I have, this very afternoon, sent letters to Sir Anthony Denny at Cheshunt, one of your father's gentlemen at court. He and his wife will welcome you tomorrow at Cheshunt."

I said nothing. Nothing was expected of me.

"God has given you great qualities, Elizabeth. Cultivate them always. And labor to improve them, for I believe you are destined, by heaven, to be Queen of England. Now you may rise and take your leave and oversee the packing, which your maids have already begun."

I rose. I kissed her. I thanked her. And I left the room.

I felt cold, abandoned, put out. But I said nothing. I had brought it all upon myself. Of course Sir Tom had brought a lot of it down on my head too, but I couldn't bring myself to blame him.

Sir Tom left before I did. The next morning I was taking breakfast alone in my room, as Cat Ashley had suggested, when I heard a commotion outside. I went to the large multi-paned window and looked down. There was a bevy of men of all stripes on horseback, two carriages full of possessions, and Sir Tom, mounted on his favorite horse, with all his dogs beside him, ready to ride off.

He was doing the work of his title as Lord Admiral, going to some island, maybe the Scillies.

He rode off with a great clatter, raising dust all about, without even saying good-bye to me.

It was a warm, dusty day in early June. I rode my own horse rather than ride in the coach with Cat Ashley and Mr. Parry. I did not want to be preached at. The Vernon brothers rode on either side of me. And except for the disgrace I'd left

74

behind me, it could have been a gay outing. We rode through the countryside and people came out of their houses to cheer us on.

Some of them threw flowers. At some places I stopped, to the dismay of my knights, who could scarce keep the people away from me.

In one village there was a country fair, and the Vernon brothers agreed I could stop but not get off my horse. One lady brought me a meat pie, which I ate astride while people stared and shouted, "God save Princess Elizabeth."

An elderly man came up to me and put his hand on my horse's reins, and immediately Richard Vernon was there, hand on his sword hilt, pushing his horse in the way. "Away from the Princess," he ordered.

"I just want to tell her something," he protested feebly.

"It's all right, Richard, leave him be. What is it, sir?" I asked.

"The people don't have work," he told me in a whispery voice. "If they do, they receive too little. Prices are too dear, and when you purchase something it's of shabby value. Feather beds are stuffed with rubbish. There is a new law against being unemployed that makes it legal for vagabonds and their children to be sold into slavery."

I nodded, listening intently. "I'll tell my brother, the King," I said.

He shouted more troubling things at me as we rode off. "There are brigands roaming the countryside and stealing the sheep and whatever we have of value. The crops are poor this year."

It seemed I could hear his voice, weak and appealing, in my head, long after we left him.

*What if I were Queen?* I thought. *What would I do about feather beds stuffed with rubbish? Mustn't a Queen care about such goings-on in her kingdom? How could I keep all my people happy?*

A haunting crescent moon was rising above the woodlands as we approached the stone manor called Cheshunt. Through the thick foliage that seemed to protect the place I could see distant torchlights shining and vague shadows waiting. My knights rode on ahead. As we began the approach to the manor I saw how it rose in the moonlight, with peaks and turrets and blank windows, with shadows of trees splashed on the terrace, with the smell of roses coming from inside the courtyard. Dogs came to greet us, sniffing and wagging their tails.

I felt a sense of peace overtake me as I dismounted. My whole household got down off their horses and out of the wagons, and the servants started to unpack my things.

This looked like the perfect place to lick my wounds. To soothe my heart after Sir Thomas's betrayal of me the day we were caught in the garden. Though I knew I could never forget how he'd flung himself at Katharine's feet and made me out a wanton, perhaps here I could put a new perspective on it. And here I could also properly mourn the death of my old tutor, Mr. Grindal, which I had been unable to do in all the commotion back at Chelsea.

The Dennys were on the marble front steps, waiting, more servants lined up behind them. "Welcome to Cheshunt," Sir Anthony Denny said. He was a short, fat man with a balding head. His wife looked like my Cat Ashley, and as she and the maids curtseyed to me, I could see over their heads to the large, cool interior of the house, where paintings hung on the walls and tapestries draped the windows and Persian carpets graced the floors.

*This is my world now,* I told myself. Sir Tom and Katharine and Lady Jane seemed far away. *My household. I am in charge.*

I was fifteen, a woman. And I was determined, from here on in, to act like one.


Denny showed me the gallery first thing the next morning. It was his collection, his doing, he said proudly. And so we walked through the great hall to the solarium above, where he pointed out a painting of my grandfather Henry VII.

"Not only a King," Denny told me, "but a businessman and warrior. He ran the kingdom with a tight purse. Yet he fought against Richard the King at Bosworth Field to take the throne like a true warrior. And so founded the mighty Tudors."

My grandfather did not look like a warrior. More like a keeper of monies, like Mr. Parry. But one could never tell what was behind quiet eyes and a modest expression.

"And here, your father." He pointed to a painting that

brought to life all my memories. The massive trunk of a body, the fine set of the head under the familiar velvet hat with the feather, the bejeweled hands, the commanding expression.

"Your father was a great King. But to his own sorrow, he has but one son."

I thought of Edward, my brother. I thought of his persistent cough.

"You are a true bairn of your father," he told me. "We are honored to have you here. I am honored to serve her who may be England's future Queen."

And he bowed. Then righted himself. "Except, of course, that I am sorry for the sickness at Chelsea that killed your tutor and threatened your house."

The sweating sickness. Of course! That was the reason Katharine had probably told him I was coming.

"Does not my father have another son?" I asked him. For I had heard of the boy Henry Darnley, a grand-nephew of my father's, whose mother was a Countess. But I had never seen him.

"Yes, and he thrives, strong and handsome."

"And will he someday make a claim to the throne?"

"I think not. Not while there exists a you. And a Mary. But you must be careful, Princess. For much depends on the man you marry."

The man I marry! Did he know about Sir Tom and me, then? Was he warning me? This man knew much about my family, I told myself. After all, he had served on my father's privy council. I must be discreet around him.

"Are you satisfield with your rooms, Princess?" he asked me.

"Yes. Everything is lovely."

"We had short notice. Adjustments can always be made. And your tutor must feel free to ask favors also."

"Thank you, Sir Anthony. I think I shall return to my rooms now."

Perhaps a little more discretion around all would be the path to follow.

For the first week I did as I pleased. I read and walked in the gardens and played with the dogs at Cheshunt. I rode, with James and Richard Vernon and Sir John Chertsey as escorts. I watched them joust and practice archery and swordplay.

My Cat Ashley told me that my tutor wanted to start lessons, so I should take my leisure while I could. She did not know that my lessons *were* my leisure, another form of leisure, wherein I could lose myself in Cicero, Sallust, Aesop; in rich, soothing Latin; in musical French. And speaking of music, I knew we'd be practicing dancing, the virginals, the flute.

Soon my lessons began. And so, in my chamber of a morning, with the windows open to the July and August sunshine, with the sounds of the farm animals and the chirping of birds, I would sit with Roger Ascham.

He took his job seriously, though he was not serious. He

now wore, as if we were starting a new era of learning, a dusty black robe and fustian cap. His black curls were long now and he left them that way.

"Sir, I have neglected my studies," I said. "We must put aside all pleasure and bow our heads to the task."

He grinned. "Nicely put, madam, but I thought your studies *were* pleasure."

"Shall we read Horace today, Master?" I asked. "I am in need of some poetry."

And so we got back to work. And so I took pleasure in it. And so, for hours at a time, at least, I did not think of Sir Tom. Or wonder about Katharine's baby.

The first week of September, a rider came up the lane, breathless, with a message. Katharine had given birth to a baby girl, and mother and baby were doing well.

The note was from Tom, who'd gotten home just in time for the birth. I stared at the parchment in my hand, stared at his signature, wondered that he'd actually written to me. He seemed so far away, so much a part of my past, yet the signature and the fact that he'd touched this very paper quickened me. I felt tears in my eyes. *Oh Tom,* I thought, *what's to become of us? Will we ever see each other again?*

Did I want to? He'd betrayed me, the day he shoved me off his lap and told Katharine he was just trying to comfort me because of Mr. Grindal's dying.

But I still had some feeling for him. If he had come

through the door at that moment, I would have trembled and run to him. And I hated myself for it.

Mornings, we worked at Greek and Latin, afternoons mathematics. Another week went by, and then one dark night another rider came up to the house with a message.

I could not have borne it if Mr. Ascham had not been by my side.

Katharine had died from childbed fever after giving birth and being delirious for days. The letter was from Lady Jane. I held it in my hand, not wanting to believe it. My heart wrung for Katharine. I refused to believe she was dead, and collapsed in Roger Ascham's arms.

I did not go to the funeral, even though it was the first Protestant royal funeral ever held in England. I heard that Lady Jane was the chief female mourner so I wanted to stay away. There was nothing I could do, and I did not want to see Sir Tom. And I would not send a note of condolence to him, as Cat Ashley wanted. She had to send it instead.

I could not bear to go to the funeral of the woman I had wronged in spite of all her kindness to me. And, as it turned out, she had left me half her personal jewels. I warmed to the thought that this meant she had forgiven me.

The leaves blew off the trees and the wind wrapped the manor house in cold. The days lost their color so that everything was painted in different shades of gray. Fireplaces were lighted throughout the house. Hot mulled wine was served at dinner. The dogs came into the house and gathered round the hearth at night. We existed, a world unto ourselves.

Right before Christmas he came to see me. Cat Ashley came to the sun-filled room upstairs where I was reading Greek with Mr. Ascham.

"The Lord High Admiral is here to see you, my lady."

I felt my face burn, as it did whenever she or Mr. Parry spoke of him. And they spoke of him often in my presence.

"Did he ask for me?" I tried to make my voice sound casual.

"Yes. He is waiting downstairs to see you."

"Tell him I have a fever. I can't come down."

Cat Ashley frowned and shook her head.

"Why is he here?" I asked before she left the room.

"He is consulting with Mr. Parry about your lands, your holdings, your accounts," she said.

*As a suitor would,* I thought to myself. And still I refused to go down to meet him.

After she left, Mr. Ascham looked at me with those gentle brown eyes of his. "Playing the coquette?" he asked.

"I can't," I said. "I can't see him."

"I've heard he's a dashing hero of a man, involved in everything. A man for the new times, as I consider myself to be. Don't be hard on him, Bess." Leave it to one man to defend another.

He called me "Bess" in only the most intimate moments. I went back to my Greek. Outside, through the large glass window, I saw Sir Tom and his men riding away.

## CHAPTER NINE

"*O*h, and he would make you a good husband," Cat Ashley said as she combed my hair the next morning. "He is tall and handsome and so involved in important matters. And he is uncle to the King."

"As I am sister to the King," I reminded her.

"If the Protector and council give their consent, you should wed him. He loves you. He told Mr. Parry he would press his suit if you encouraged him."

"I have some feeling left for him too, Pussy Cat," I answered, using my pet name for her, "but there is more at stake than that."

"What? What could possibly deter you?"

*That I may someday be Queen,* I thought. *His own dear wife, Katharine, told me so. And as Queen, I must be careful of whom I wed. Sir Tom has not shown me many strong attributes, for me to want to make him my King.* But I didn't say it aloud, for fear of being labeled brazen by Cat Ashley.

I had already decided I would never wed any man. Sir Tom had broken my heart. He had been partially responsible for my disgrace. He had rendered me helpless. And then there was my own indignation. How dare he make me suffer, turn me this way and then that, like a puppet, and then come back to me again and expect me to marry him?

I vowed I would never let any man so turn my world upside down again.

She finished my hair. I put on my cap. "I'm going riding with Mr. Ascham this morning," I told her. "It's Saturday. There are no lessons."

I got sick soon after. I came down with some malady that the doctors could not put a name to. The top of my head felt as if rocks were piled on it. I was weak and could scarce get about. My nose was runny and my lungs felt inflamed. So I stayed abed, obediently taking all the potions from the local apothecary that the doctors had ordered and providing fresh fuel for the fire of the rumors that were circulating about me. My serving girls told me everything they overheard at the apothecary.

The rumor went that I was pregnant with Sir Tom's child, and that was why I was hiding out at Cheshunt.

It got even better. There was a renowned midwife, they said, who was wakened from her sleep in the middle of the night to be blindfolded and taken on a horse to a manor house deep in the woods, where she was asked to deliver a baby of a woman with flaming red hair. The baby was delivered and carried off, never to be seen again.

Well, I thought, at least I am providing story fodder for people to be entertained with around their fires on cold winter nights.

Cat Ashley blamed my malady on everything but the truth. The manor house, she said, was too close to a large marshland. The new surroundings at Cheshunt were full of vapors in the air that poisoned me. I was growing too fast. I was not growing fast enough. I was eating too much, not eating enough. I had never had a mother and now that I was becoming a woman I needed one more than ever before.

She saw everything but the obvious. I was lovesick for Sir Thomas and I hated him at the same time. My insides were in a turmoil over what to make of this.

My malady lasted four weeks, then disappeared as quickly as it had come. We were now into December. I became homesick for Hatfield, house of my childhood. I asked Mr. Parry, who was about to go to London to see about my estates, if he would visit the King and entreat him to allow me to go home.

I knew Edward would also remember Hatfield as a place where we had enjoyed good times as children. Perhaps even he longed for it. Mr. Parry came back in a week and sat down in my chamber next to my bed. In his hands were pages of official-looking parchment.

"Do you know the full extent of your holdings, Princess?" he asked.

"No."

"Then let me read them off to you." And he proceeded to tell me all that I owned since my father's death.

"These are letters patent," he said, "finally assuring to Your Grace all the properties mentioned in your father's will. There are dozens of manor houses to the immediate northwest of London. One group is in Oxfordshire. Another circles around Ashridge. You now own one of your childhood homes on the Buckinghamshire-Hertfordshire border, your own Berkhamsted, Hemel Hempstead, and in this grant are the towns of Princes Risborough and Missenden."

"All that?" I gaped.

"And more, Princess. You now own Collyweston, the great country palace of your great-grandmother Lady Margaret Beaufort. There are estates and manors in Huntingdonshire, a group of manors across the Rutland border, lands in Newbury. There are estates in Dorset, Hampshire, and Lincolnshire. And you own Durham Place in London. It is your town palace. Shall I go on?" He shuffled the parchments.

"No. I'm breathless. Only tell me one thing, Mr. Parry."

"Yes, Your Grace."

"Did my brother say I could go back to Hatfield?"

Permission had been given. I could go as soon as I wanted.

So I had my maids pack. And taking advantage of the

frozen ground, we set out two weeks before Christmas to go home to Hatfield. There were tears when we departed, of course. Sir Anthony Denny and his wife cried unashamedly and gave advice the same way.

"Be careful of all men," from Sir Anthony.

"Study hard and keep your household well," from his wife.

I thanked them for taking me in, for I had indeed been a waif in sore need of parental figures when I came. And they had played their parts well.

Hatfield! We approached in the starkness of winter, with bright blue skies and all the oak trees bare around the place, with gold light bathing its brick façade. Everything was frozen and so every line of it stood out and reached into my very heart. I had been a child here. Here I had run and played with Edward and Lady Jane and Robin. Robin! Would I ever see him again? Was he still alive?

The old house embraced me. Servants stood just inside the courtyard, and from here I could survey my whole world, it seemed. Inside, bright fires crackled. Tables were laden with sweetmeats and hot mulled cider. Dogs came over to greet me, remembering me and wagging their tails.

We kept Christmas at Hatfield that year instead of going to court. At Hatfield I felt safe. There the rumors couldn't touch me. There, there were no ghosts of Sir Tom or Katharine.

There I could start new.

I sent my gentlemen and yeomen out into the woods to collect red holly-berry branches and evergreens to decorate the place, chestnuts to roast. They went gladly. Then, just as gladly, my knights helped me decorate. After that they went hunting with Roger Ascham for the Yuletide dinner. I put cloth of gold and velvet ribbons on everything, from newel posts to clocks.

We prepared a Yuletide feast that would do my father proud.

My yeomen cut a Yule log and some applewood, and soon the fragrances of applewood, evergreen, and chestnuts permeated the whole house.

The week before Christmas he came.

He came riding up in the snow, with his men around him, brandishing a sword. With his dark, swirling cloak, his torso clad in an embroidered velvet doublet, and ruffles at his neck and wrists, he seemed to me a mixture of Christopher Columbus, Richard III, and Saint George right before he slew the dragon.

I received him in the large front hall. I curtseyed and he bowed, and I frowned at Cat Ashley to send her from the room.

"So we're alone at last," he said.

I was trembling. The nearness of him near drove me to distraction. He loomed over me, with the outside aromas he carried, of horse and fresh air and leather.

He lighted his clay pipe, adding another lingering male aroma to the rest. We sat. I tendered my sorrow for Katharine's death. He said the baby was fine and I told him

I'd heard he had broken up his household and sent Lady Jane home.

"Yes. Poor little waif. She thinks she has done something to offend me. I will put my household together again and bring her back, with my mother in charge. If only . . ." His voice trailed off.

"If only what?" I asked.

"If only you would wed me, Elizabeth. I would love you for all of my days, and care for you."

*Like you loved Katharine?* I wanted to ask. But I could not. He was a rascal, that was a known fact. But part of me—the part in every girl that loved rascals—still did love him. I knew that when he left me today, the world would turn cold. As to marriage, the large commitment of it fell over me like a storm cloud. What would become of us? I asked him. Where would we live? His answers were addled. He seemed uncertain.

Was there any truth to the rumors that he was having to do with pirates?

"What pirates?" he asked innocently.

"Jack Thompson." I had heard the rumor and knew how rumors hurt, Lord knows. But he only smiled.

"The whole country is in ferment," I told him solemnly. "The privy council argue amongst themselves. There were attempted uprisings in many counties last spring. Anything you do will be scrutinized, but you do what you wish, always. You are known to have several irons in the fire at all times. You get into trouble and expect your charm to get you out of it. You have made an enemy of your own brother, who runs the country."

"By my faith, I see you have been doing your homework as future Queen," he said.

"Roger Ascham keeps me informed. He said I must be."

"You will not marry me, then," he said quietly.

So I said what women have been saying for years. "I will think on it."

Those were perhaps the wisest words I've ever said in my life. For now I had another consideration: my many land holdings. Was he after them? Certainly he knew of them. He had offered Mr. Parry his services in "settling my estates."

I did not feel very wise at the time. I felt lost and confused and upside down, so I did what I always do when I was perplexed about something. I went for a ride with my knights, through the woods and across the white, snow-covered fields of Hatfield. The sky was robin's-egg blue, the sun warm on my face, the wind cleansing, and the world delicious and new after the snow. Everything sparkled. Deer ran across our path. Rabbits scurried. Squirrels chattered. *Life could be so simple,* I thought, turning and looking at the vast expanse of red brick and sparkling windows that was Hatfield. *Why can't my life be?*

# CHAPTER TEN

We got back from our ride, exhilarated and joking, to see a bevy of strange horses in the front courtyard. I stared.

The horses wore the green and white of my brother's court. My heart jumped. Was something wrong with Edward, the King?

In the great chamber, my main reception room where my gentlemen and yeomen waited as guards of honor, they were now standing, alert and none too happy looking.

"What is it?" I asked as one of my ladies helped remove my purple velvet riding habit. "What has happened?"

There was a whole contingent of the Protector's men, armed and with the stoniest of faces. Their leader, a tall, dark-scowling man, turned and bowed.

It was Sir Robert Tyrwhitt, who had once been Katharine's Master of Horse.

"What is the meaning of this?" came the loud demanding voice of Richard Vernon. "How dare you come into the Princess's house armed?"

Immediately he and his brother, James, and Sir John Chertsey placed themselves around me protectively.

Sir Robert held up a scroll. "Princess Elizabeth, I am ordered by the King and the council to seize two of your servants and place them under arrest. I will take them with me now."

"My servants? Who? Why?"

"Catherine Ashley and Thomas Parry, your accounting officer."

Mr. Parry, Cat Ashley, and Roger Ascham had just entered the room. One of the soldiers grabbed Cat Ashley's arm and two others held Mr. Parry. Cat Ashley's face went white. She was trembling. Mr. Parry, good man that he was, seemed confused. I reached a hand out to them and my knights started forward, but I held them back as my two servants were pulled out of the house.

Behind me I heard Roger Ascham saying, "Good lord, is this Edward's new regime, then?"

The front door slammed. My dogs were in the hallway, barking. There was no other sound for a moment or two, and then a clattering of horses' hooves as they rode away.

The silence in the place was like a rebuke. How could such a thing happen? The Vernon brothers and Sir John

Chertsey felt denied their right to protect me.

"We could have driven them off, my lady," said Sir John.

"No, no, something is going on. Something is not right. Leave me now—I must think."

All left but Roger Ascham.

"They'll take them to the Tower," I moaned. "Through Traitor's Gate. Oh, my Pussy Cat won't be able to abide it."

"Come, Princess, mayhap you ought to rest. There will be no more lessons today."

Obediently, accompanied by two of my maids, I went to my chamber, thinking grimly, *I think, Roger, that the lessons are just beginning.*

Over the next two days I made a feeble attempt at study. But in the middle of a lesson on penmanship or translating Greek, I would stare off into space and say to Roger, "I want to talk about Pussy Cat and Mr. Parry. What could they have done? Help me to think through it."

And so we would talk it through, all the while Roger reassuring me, making perfect sense out of his conjecture. I would believe his positive assessment one moment and in the next plunge into the dark hole of fear inside me.

"Edward, the King, is your brother," Roger would say. "He won't let anything happen to you or your people."

"Suppose Mr. Parry has not been honest with my accounts?"

We both agreed that was probably the problem.

"You must learn to think and act like a Queen," Roger

told me. "It is now, if ever, that your education will see you through."

Without Roger I would have perished. When there was no more talk in us, he would take me out for a ride in the bracing cold with my knights.

"Your actions must always be Queenly," he kept telling me.

In two days Sir Robert Tyrwhitt came for me.

He came with a body of men, armed soldiers and servants. Fortunately my knights were in the dining hall out back when he came, or they would have died on the spot protecting me.

He came with a writ from the council, which he read to me as I stood with two of my maids in the great hall. "Princess Elizabeth, I am ordered by the council of our lord and King, Edward, to seize upon you. By the power invested in me I do arrest you now on the charge of high treason."

My whole body got cold, but my face got hot. I felt rather than saw a presence slip beside me. Roger Ascham. Then I remembered his words. "Act like a Queen, always."

I could not swallow. I cleared my throat and Sir Robert went on. "It is also my duty to inform you that the Lord High Admiral has just been arrested by order of the council and taken to the Tower."

I found my voice, and made sure it was clear and full of contempt. "By what right does the council accuse me of treason?"

He smiled. Does a scorpion smile? He looked like a

scorpion. "Did you not have an affair with Sir Thomas Seymour at Chelsea?"

My head was spinning. *Think like a Queen.*

"No. I did not."

"Did you not know that constitutes treason? For him and for you?"

"I have not commited treason," I replied.

"Your Mr. Parry and Catherine Ashley are singing a different tune in the Tower right now. It is strange what the mind can remember when the body is threatened with death, isn't it?" Another grin from the scorpion.

I felt Roger move closer to me.

"I am second in line for the throne," I said. "How dare you speak to me this way?"

"I have the authority of the throne behind me," he said.

"Don't bully me," I said. "I remind you, I may be Queen someday, and I will remember it if you do."

That quieted Sir Robert somewhat, though it did not stop him from ordering his men to encircle the house, to confiscate the weapons, to herd the house servants into one room and guard them, to round up my knights and yeomen and do likewise. He gave Roger Ascham the choice of going to his rooms or staying with the servants.

Sir Robert would question me this day. He would not leave until he got the answers he wanted. And he would begin here and now.

He bade me sit. The fire in the great hall was crackling when he began and near ashes when he stopped. I was given neither food nor drink nor anyone to stay with me. It was just he and I, alone.

He took the superior position, pacing back and forth in front of where I was seated, as if I were on trial.

Questioning.

"Did you not promise not to marry until you got the permission of the council and the Protector?"

"I had no intention of marrying, sir."

"Not Sir Thomas Seymour? He came around seeking Mr. Parry's advice about your estates. Is that not true?"

"Yes. But I had naught to do with it."

"Did he ask you to wed him?"

"Yes."

"And what did you say?"

"I did not agree to wed anybody."

"Did you know about his plan to kidnap your brother and set up another government?"

I gasped. "No."

"He broke into your brother's rooms while he was sleeping. He shot your brother's dog and attempted to kidnap him. He has had dealings with false coinage and with pirates, in particular with Black Jack. He has promised their ships safe conduct in return for a portion of the spoils, and he has arrested the captains of the Royal Navy who will not give these thugs safe conduct. As if all that weren't enough, he tried to kidnap the King to set up his own government with himself as Protector. He's had the chief counter of the Royal Mint, a man named Sherrington, shaving off gold coins for a year to accumulate four thousand pounds' worth to finance his rebellion. He has men, guns, powder, plans, and an armory at Holt Castle. It has been discovered by spies."

*Oh, Tom, Tom,* I thought. *You always were rash. But this!* I tried to keep a stoic expression on my face.

"And did you not carry on an affair with him at Chelsea before his wife died?" Sir Robert persisted.

"No. I took part in no such affair."

"My wife was one of the ladies-in-waiting for Queen Katharine and she heard about the carrying-on. Do you say my wife is a liar?"

"Sir, your esteemed wife may have heard false information. There were many rumors thrown around about me."

"What would you say if I told you that Mrs. Ashley and Mr. Parry both admitted to this under questioning?"

"I would say you frightened them into submission."

Oh, I would not live through this. I was trembling.

When the fire was low and the great hall was chilled, he called for a servant to bring wood, to bring him some supper. And he ate there in front of me, offering me nothing.

The questioning went on until all the great clocks chimed twelve midnight. Then he rose and said I was to go to bed. No, I could not have my own maids. He went out into the hall and called for someone, and an old hag of a limping woman came in and accompanied me upstairs. She smelled of the barnyard and I thought I saw bugs crawling in her hair. Did Sir Robert do this to me intentionally, to break me? Of course! *But I won't break,* I promised myself. *I will act like a Queen.*

I was under arrest. It was a temporary situation, after all. I supposed he must treat me so. I fell into a fitful sleep, thinking of Pussy Cat and Mr. Parry in the Tower.

When I was allowed out of my chamber the next morning, I saw that the house was full of soldiers, coming and going as they pleased, dirtying the place with their soiled boots, smirking at my maids, and ready to start fights with my knights, who stood loyally in the great hall, ready to fight to the death for me.

Roger Ascham was nowhere in sight.

Sir Robert questioned me for two days, during which I had to use all of my wits to stay ahead of him. Several times I told him: "I have done nothing. How can I be charged?"

Once he asked me: "What would you say if I told you they are about to execute Sir Tom?"

"I would say that if they give him a fair trial and he is proved guilty, so be it."

But inside I was dying. Take Tom's head from his shoulders? As had been done to my mother? Sir Robert had known the effect that would have upon me. He was watching my face closely.

"It appears the council is denying him an open trial. They have drawn up a bill of attainder. Have you anything else to say, Princess Elizabeth?"

A bill of attainder, a definite conclusion of his guilt. "Yes. I'm hungry. I haven't eaten for two days. And I'm concerned over the welfare of my people. Where is my tutor? Where are my knights? Your soldiers have tramped all through my house. It smells of horses and men."

My show of strength, my quick thinking, my wits had impressed him. He told me that the written confessions of Cat Ashley and Mr. Parry were exactly alike. They told of my being smitten with Sir Tom, of my and his sexual play in my chamber, of the day Katharine caught me on his lap, kissing. But they told no more.

They told no more because there was no more to tell. Mr. Parry and Cat Ashley both had been threatened with torture, shown thumb screws and other instruments of pain, so their confessions were believed to be the truth.

There was nothing in the confessions to connect either them or me to Sir Tom's conspiracy to overthrow the government.

"I see no definite proof of treason," Sir Robert said.

Shortly after that he withdrew. He left with his men and horses and I had to gather my trembling self. Both Roger Ascham and William Grindal had taught me that the truth always solves matters. And so now, inwardly, I thanked them.

I dressed myself in a deep blue-colored velvet gown. Over it I put a stiff stomacher. There were separate lace sleeves and at least fifty tiny buttons on the front of the gown. I struggled, dressing myself, but I must do it. Then I put on my ruby cross and went downstairs and like a Queen, set my maids about cleaning and sweetening the house. I ordered applewood fires and the fragrance of lilac for my chamber. I ordered a dinner to be cooked for myself and Roger Ascham and my knights, of my favorite foods. I was starving, though I could scarce eat. I awaited word of my Pussy Cat and Mr. Parry.

Before he left, Sir Robert had made a parting shot by telling me that there was a rumor about that I was pregnant with Tom's child. After dinner I wrote in anger to the Protector, telling him to have this rumor put down, that it was slander to my family name as sister to the King and daughter of Henry VIII. And that I must see my brother, Edward.

I finally got permission to go. I arrived at the palace on a windy, cloudy March day, my knights and yeomen accompanying me. But there was no Pussy Cat Ashley to comfort or encourage me, and my maids could not fill that role.

I found Edward in his presence chamber, surrounded by his squires and servants, his maps and telescopes, his magnetic needle and astrolabe. He loved comets and rainbows. He loved to talk about the New World and sending ships out to explore.

"Make way for the sister of the King!"

"Elizabeth!" He reached out a slender hand.

Oh, he'd gotten so tall! At eleven his face had thinned so that the jawline defined a troubled youth. His eyes seemed over-large and mournful. I knelt at his feet and he raised me up and hugged me, and I felt in the hug all the longing and fear he was feeling.

He sent his men from the room so we could be alone.

"The matter you wrote to the Protector about has been

taken care of," he told me. "The rumors are quelled. I am sorry you had to endure all that, Elizabeth, but your name had to be cleared."

"Edward, are they going to execute Tom?"

"I am afraid so."

"But can't you stop it?"

"I think, right now, that the Protector himself couldn't stop his brother's execution," he told me. "Tom was going to kidnap me. He shot my dog, Elizabeth. He poisoned Katharine. You know how I loved Katharine."

"I don't think he did that, Edward. It's a vicious rumor."

"Well, of course you wouldn't believe it. You loved him. But I dare not go against the council or my Protector. And I wish you would separate yourself from Thomas, Elizabeth. He wanted to overthrow my government. There was treason!"

"What about Cat Ashley and Mr. Parry? Will you let them out of the Tower?"

"Ah," he said, "two foolish but lovable people. I know they told the truth. And my uncle Tom, when questioned, never implicated you or them in his schemes."

"You will let them go, then?"

"For you, yes."

We hugged again, and I felt the tremendous burden of loving anyone bearing down inside me.

On the twentieth of March they beheaded Thomas Seymour. His brother, the Protector, did not go to the execution. They said that on Thomas's last night he wrote two secret letters, one to me and one to my sister, Mary. I never received one. Neither did she. But we were told the contents. In the letters was an admonition to "overthrow the Protector and bring him to the same end."

Tom gone. A dashing, handsome courtier, full of devilment and laughter and at the business of breaking women's hearts every day. That's how I had first seen him. But he had another side—a scheming, dishonest side—that dealt in betrayal every day.

How could such a force be gone from the earth? Despite all that I had learned about him, I could not accept it. I fell into doldrums, with headaches and body aches and loss of appetite. And then, one fine day in June, two things happened.

Roger Ascham leaned forward across the table in the middle of my lessons and asked my permission to take a sabbatical. "I'd like to travel abroad for a while," he said. "I need to fill up my soul with wisdom. You are grown now, Princess. You are becoming wiser than I. I need to replenish my mind so I can continue to teach you. I am drying up here."

I never thought of Roger as having a mind that could "dry up." But I did wonder sometimes how he could teach all day, five days a week, and never stop talking and reasoning and conjecturing.

"I give my permission," I said in as dignified manner as I could. "But I shall miss you."

"You have just come through a tremendous crisis with all the aplomb and wisdom of a Queen," he said. "You can do without me for a while. I shall miss you too."

On that same day, Cat Ashley and Mr. Parry came back to me.

She begged my forgiveness after a moment or two of hugging. "For what?" I asked.

"For not standing by you. For talking. For telling them about . . ." Her voice trailed off.

"There is nothing to forgive," I told her. And him. "We have all come through some dreadful nightmare and we must now rest and heal."

Pussy Cat told me about her dank cell, about her jailer, a man who treated her well, and about how she had constantly "asked for you, Princess. I think my position as your nurse saved me much pain in prison."

Mr. Parry told me about Richard Rich, the Chief Inquisitor. "He is known to be the most devious and heartless they have," Mr. Parry said. "They made us talk; they showed us the rack and thumb screws. I am sorry."

"You told the truth," I assured them both. "And it was just that. And it didn't amount to treason."

A moment later, our first moment alone, Pussy Cat looked at me. "My lady," she said, "you have grown up. You are a little girl no longer."

There was fear in her face. I was not yet sixteen.

# CHAPTER ELEVEN

*I*n spite of myself, I went into weeks of brooding after Sir Thomas's death. I put aside my silks and velvets and wore white, plain and simple, that summer. I developed crippling headaches again and took to my bed. Cat did not know what to do with me so she tiptoed around my chamber making clucking noises and calling me "child," she who had said I was finally grown up.

I also missed Roger Ascham and his quiet encouragement. I could not eat and I lost weight.

Sir Tom. I could not stop thinking of him, of the way he had made me feel. He had been convicted of three and thirty counts of high treason. He'd been accused of having ten thousand men ready for an insurrection.

He had not died well, they said. He made no last-minute

speech, he did not ask for forgiveness, he did not bless the King. He had to be dragged to the block on Tower Green and went to his death fighting his jailers to the last.

"Never again," I told myself once more. "Never again will I let any man hold sway over me."

It was 1549. Four months went by with my scarcely seeing anyone except members of my household. To lift my spirits, Edward sent me some household gifts, mostly tapestries. Twenty-one pieces in all, five showing hunting and hawking scenes and four with the history of Hercules, others with scenes from the Bible. He sent me dozens of Turkish carpets, a rich bed canopy with matching curtains, two chairs upholstered in cloth of gold and red velvet, and thirteen velvet and embroidered cushions for window seats.

To accommodate these new furnishings we redecorated Hatfield. I had the great chamber that was the main reception room refurbished. It was where my knights and yeomen spent their time, as guards of honor. The same was done to the presence chamber, where I received important visitors. The place needed a new face inside and I thought perhaps it would brighten things.

It came to me from those I had spying for me at court that my marriage was under discussion.

The proposals came in, one after another.

The French Duke of Guise wanted me to marry his brother. To appease the court I sat for a portrait and had it sent to the young man, only to hear no response.

The Dukes of Ferrara and Florence also tendered their wish to become betrothed to me, but one was only eleven years old.

All were Catholic.

Then came the offer from the King of Denmark's eldest son. The council agreed to go into negotiations with this one. But I stayed silent, neither objecting nor expressing interest. I had no intention of marrying anybody and these offers always came to nothing.

Then a letter came from my sister, whom I seldom heard from anymore. "There is a disturbance going on with the council," she wrote. "John Dudley, the Earl of Warwick, is wrestling with the Lord Protector to take over power. If contacted by either, do not give your blessing to either one or get involved."

I received a letter from the Lord Protector, asking me not to side with the Earl of Warwick, who was Robin's father. But I did not respond, and inwardly I thanked Mary for the warning. Writing my thanks to her would be too dangerous, and she would know that.

So, the Dudleys were back in court. And Robin's father was fighting for the place of Protector.

I went about my business, losing myself in my beloved Hatfield and my own life. Mr. Parry was teaching me to go over my account books faithfully.

"You are living very economically," he praised me. "Your table is supplied by your estates. Your huntsmen and farmers are supplying all the partridge, veal, beef, and poultry, all the eggs, wheat, barley, and oats for your horses. And some messenger is always coming to the back gate with presents from the people."

"I know." I smiled. "Yesterday someone delivered a plump swan. The kitchen people are roasting it today."

"Your sister spends more than you," he advised. "You have the means, Elizabeth; you ought to indulge yourself a little. Do you need new clothes? How about entertainers? You are old enough now to put on entertainments and invite some of the local noblemen and their families."

It was 1551. On September seventh I would be eighteen. "I'll put on an entertainment for my birthday," I told him. "Cat Ashley and I will plan it."

And so I did. I did not invite anyone from court, which included any of the Dudley brothers, but I did invite some of the local noblemen and their families who had been sending me gifts all along.

I hired Master John Heywood's Troupe of Child Performers, and for music, I engaged Farmor the lutist, More the harper, and Lord Russell's minstrels. And because I wanted to play the lute myself, at my party, I spent seventeen shillings replacing lutestrings.

The party was a success. Mr. Parry gave me power to take over the books and spend as I wished, and I began to feel more grown up.

I gave Cat Ashley money for Holland cloth for new towels. I paid a carpenter to make a walnut table for my study in exactly the shape I wanted. I increased my alms for the poor.

And I still rode out with my knights and hunted when the weather allowed. It was a most beautiful fall.

Often, as this morning in October, I thought of Robin when we were out riding. These were the same fields and woods where I'd once ridden with him, where I'd gone hawking with him and watched in admiration as his giant, gold-winged creature came out of the sky to place gentle talons on Robin's padded arm, and stand there preening, its eyes darting about, waiting for praise, a mouse or small rabbit dangling from its beak.

Why was the thought of Robin always so much with me? Because I knew he was back at court? What role was he playing in this fight of his father's? I knew he adored his father, would do anything for him.

Why didn't he write me since he was back at court? I shook the thoughts away and raised my face to the still-warm October sun and let it bathe me in its blessed peace.

"We should be quail hunting." Richard Vernon's voice brought me back to the present. "Look, Princess."

I looked. A whole bunch of quail were walking in the woods to the side of us. "Yes, but I don't want to kill anything today," I told him. "Today I want everything to live and be happy."

The Vernon brothers and Sir John Chertsey laughed, if somewhat uneasily. They, of course, knew of the beheading of Sir Tom, knew the effect it had had on me, and were likely under Cat's orders to help me mend and heal.

About twenty minutes after that, we were all raised out of our lulling mood to see a rider coming down the dusty road to the left of us. The horse, a large bay, turned into the fields and started leaping over fences, frightening some sheep, as if its rider were a madman. My heart seemed to stop for a moment. I saw my knights' hands go to the hilts of their swords as the horse raced toward us.

As the rider came close, I shielded the sun from my eyes with my hand so I could recognize him. But I could not. All I saw was the green-and-white colors of my brother's court.

*Not again!* That was all I thought. But I took some comfort in the thought that he was alone and not accompanied by soldiers.

He pulled up his horse, which was wild in the eye and did not want to stop. He held the prancing animal still while he swept off his feathered hat and bowed in the saddle.

I heard a scraping noise as my knights unsheathed their swords.

"Identify yourself, sir," said Richard Vernon.

"Elizabeth," the rider said, looking down at me.

Did I know those brown eyes? For a moment I thought I did. Then James Vernon pushed his horse between mine and the newcomer's.

"Princess Elizabeth," he corrected.

"Never mind that," said Richard. "Who are you, sir? What business have you with the Princess?"

A familiar smile broke across the young man's face. "I'm

sorry, but I never thought I would present a danger. I've known the Princess since I was three. Elizabeth, it's Robin. Robin Dudley. Don't you recognize me?"

I was surprised and not surprised all at the same time.

I had not recognized him at all at first. Then he took off his hat again and I remembered the brown curls. I could not help staring. He was Robin, my childhood friend, and he was not. He was a ghost of the childhood friend, grown fully, with the broad shoulders of a man and the courtly manners of one schooled by his powerful father and polished in court. His hands were those of a man. He wore a sword and dressed like a courtier, but his clothes were not frilled and fancy as Sir Tom's had been.

His colors were solemn, serious, except for the white-and-green sash from Edward's court. His voice was grave and sure, as was his manner. We rode ahead, starting for Hatfield. My knights kept a discreet distance behind.

"When did you get back to court," I asked, "and how?"

"We've been back for a while. My father is now the Duke of Northumberland and head of the council. Didn't you hear?"

"I heard. Why didn't you write to me?"

"I didn't want to get you involved."

"What happened?" I asked.

"The Lord Protector has fallen. My father won."

"Oh."

"The Lord Protector lost the affection of the people after he executed his brother. But there was plenty before that to lead to his downfall. The weakened power of the currency, the taking away of public lands to provide grazing for the sheep of the rich, rebellions brewing in the West Country and in East Anglia. All of this he ignored. The poor people resent the fact that he pulled down six acres of buildings on the Strand to make himself a new home. And then he fled with your brother, Edward, in tow to Windsor Castle."

"Oh, poor Edward!"

"His dignity was put upon, but he was masterful all through it. My father could have mustered the army to overcome the Lord Protector, but instead he talked him into surrender. Elizabeth, it's the first bloodless transfer of power in England in decades. All the council is behind my father now: Cranmer, Southampton, Arundel, Paulet, and Cecil."

"And so what now?"

"Lord Somerset, the former Protector, is in the Tower, where he belongs. My father, now Protector, is allowing your brother more freedom, more time to play at sports, and more spending money, and letting him have more say in matters of state. Edward is very happy. He puts his hands on his hips and imitates your father's walk. He shouts thunderous oaths."

"Oh, I can't wait to see him."

"And you shall. My father wants the King's sisters to come to court. I've come to invite you."

He grinned and I saw my childhood friend.

I smiled back, sadly. "I've had many adventures of my own, Robin."

"I know." He sobered. "Did you love him?"

"In a way I hope I shall never love a man again."

"The rumors about him and you . . . are they true?"

"Partially. But we were never really lovers."

He scowled and bit his lower lip. "I've something to tell you, Elizabeth. I want to tell you before you get to court, before anyone else tells you."

My bones seemed to freeze. "What?"

"I'm betrothed."

I felt myself go hot and then cold. "You are only seventeen."

"My older brother was this age when he was wed."

"Who is she?"

"Her name is Amy. Amy Robsart. She is the daughter of a knight. I met her at court. We're in love."

Love! I felt the world spinning around me. *Never again will I let any man hold sway over me.* My own words rose like bile in my throat. Because I loved Robin. I always had. But I had never thought about what would happen after we ceased being children.

"Elizabeth." He leaned toward me from his saddle. "I love you. I always will, and I will always protect you. But you are a royal Princess, far above me in rank. I have always known that. We can't wed. And if you become Queen, you'll be expected to marry a foreign prince and make an alliance for England. Anyway, no matter what happens, we will always be friends. And friends are more important than lovers, aren't they?"

He was begging me with those wonderful brown eyes to say yes. I nodded yes, to buy myself some time. Things were moving too fast for me.

"You will be Queen someday," he said. "And I shall always serve you."

Oh, Robin!

But he was breaking my heart, all over again, not like Tom had done, slyly and without honesty. Robin's and my love had been nourished by many chaste years, by his respect and admiration for me and mine for him. It was a different kind of love, but love it was, there inside us both, smoldering with nothing to be done about it and nothing to be tried.

Cat Ashley nearly went daft. "Court! Then you must have new clothes!"

"And it is time to have them made by a tailor," I told her. "I have been thinking on it and hear nothing but good things about Mr. Warren."

So I was allowed to hire him and order what I wanted myself.

I got new velvet cloaks, silk-lined bodices, a pair of black velvet sleeves, two French hoods and lengths of damask and blue velvet, crimson satin and silks, and linen cloth to have dresses made. I was measured for them. I bought new kirtles and yards upon yards of lace for ruffs around my neck, and soon the dresses and linens and cloaks were mine.

I was past my demure stage, my humble stage of wearing nothing but white or gray. I was ready to appear in court as the King's sister.

# CHAPTER TWELVE

*R*ight before Christmas I set out for Whitehall Palace with my own retinue of men and a hundred of the King's horses, as sent to me by Edward for escort. My arrival at the palace was elaborate, to say the least. All of the council came forward to greet me and usher me to Edward in the throne room seated under a canopy of cloth of gold-and-red velvet.

"Make way for the Princess Elizabeth, sister to the King."

I made my bows, not without noticing that my sister, Mary, sat next to the throne. I hoped she did not think I was also bowing to her.

A feast had been prepared. The King's drummers, fifers, and other musicians played. Mary was seated to the left of Edward and I to the right. The new Lord Protector sat at the other end of the glittering table with his sons, Ambrose and John, Robin's older brothers, and Robin's younger, Henry and Guilford. Robin was there with his new wife, Amy, a buxom, blond-haired girl with a cow's placid eyes.

She was not at all animated. She seldom spoke. I watched her, trying not to be envious when my Robin leaned toward her or touched her face or smoothed a bit of hair back from it. What did he see in all that blandness?

All the while Mary was watching me with her short-sighted gaze. She had aged, I decided. There were some gray strands in her mousy brown hair, and when she smiled I saw that her teeth were crooked. Her complexion was splotched too, but none of this seemed to bother her.

After supper she came toward me with velvet-wrapped packages in her hands.

"I have some gifts for you, Elizabeth."

As she leaned over to sit down I whispered my thanks for the letter of warning she had sent me about not getting involved in the council fight.

She sniffed. "I think the new Protector is the most evil of men. Worse than Lord Somerset was. He wrote asking me to back a move he wanted to make to support the old Lord Protector's impeachment before Parliament. I wouldn't even reply. And, though he pretends otherwise, I am convinced that his religious policy is against all I believe in and portends disaster for me. Here, open your presents."

"Why are you giving me gifts now?" I asked innocently.

"Simple. I forgot your birthday."

I opened the velvet packages. One present was a locket with a diamond clasp. Inside were likenesses of our father and her mother, Catherine of Aragon. I blushed. What could I say? Our father had put aside that Catherine to wed my mother.

Another gift was a brooch that I could wear pinned to my collar. It depicted Pyramus and Thisbe, lovers, sketched in amethyst. Then came the sable wrap, which she opened herself and drew out to place around my shoulders.

I thanked her politely, embarrassed. "I've brought you nothing," I said.

"I need no birthday presents. I'd just as soon forget the day. Don't you forget, I'm already thirty-four and still unmarried."

"But not without proposals," I said. "I've heard of them."

"Who? Young Edward Courtenay? He's only twenty-four and been in the Tower for most of his life, being the last of the House of Plantagenet. The poor man doesn't know how to shoot a long bow or ride a horse for his imprisonment. Of course, he *is* Catholic," she mused. "And if I were Queen I would release him; then, mayhap . . ."

Her voice trailed off.

*If I were Queen.* So she thought of it too. Thought of what she would do, the people she would favor, those she would punish.

"What about Dom Luis of Portugal?"

"The new Protector is unwilling to meet the expense of my dowry."

We were silent for a minute; then she spoke. "Have you

ever wondered," she asked, "how we could both be illegitimate? If I'm illegitimate, you're not. And if you are, then I'm not. But both?"

"Our father settled that when he drew us up in line for the throne," I told her.

She nodded. Then the music struck up again, and Robin and his wife went dancing by.

"Why do you stare so at Robin Dudley?" she asked. "I know you were children together. Can't you see he's married?"

"We're still friends," I told her.

"Haven't you had enough trouble and confusion on that score?"

It was my turn to blush. "I never see him. How could I? I'm never at court and neither is he. Since his marriage he's been living in the country at his Manor of Hemsley, near Yarmouth."

"Incidentally," she said, "I hear that Amy is terrified of public life. That she is extravagant and has numerous gowns she is too shy to wear, that she is terrible at keeping a home, a disaster with servants, and has no talent whatsoever except that she is an heiress."

I felt reassured. Did Mary know more? I asked but she shook her head. Then Edward came over to join us. "Ah, my two favorite sisters," he joked. We talked awhile, the three of us. Edward told me that he'd had a letter from Roger Ascham, that my tutor was at the Council of Trent. We talked about everything except religion, and when he got up to leave, being needed across the room, Mary looked at me. "You are his favorite," she said, "not I."

"I don't think that, Mary."

"Well, can't you see the tension between us? One of these days it's going to come out in the open, our argument over religion. Protestantism is the official religion of England these days. He can't bear that I won't embrace it. He knows that I have six chaplains in my household and celebrate Mass every day. If not for the Emperor of Spain demanding that the council allow me the freedom to practice my faith, I don't know what would happen to me. Remember, he wants to keep good relations with Catholic Spain, and my mother came from there."

The visit turned out to be exhausting on account of Mary. I was never sure what to say to her or what she would say to me. One minute she was like a pussy cat, the next a tiger, and all the while I was there I prayed she and our brother, the King, would not come to blows over religion.

I stayed in the palace for Christmas and for a few weeks afterward. Then I collected my people and went back to Hatfield to find some peace.

On the twenty-second of January, 1552, Lord Somerset, the old Protector, was beheaded on Tower Hill, much as his brother had been before him. He went to his death with dignity, walking proudly to the block and blessing the King. And after the deed was done the crowd surged forward in hopes of dipping their handkerchiefs in his blood, because for some strange reason, their mood had changed and they now considered him to be a martyr.

In March I went to court again, this time riding in with a great number of lords, knights, and gentlemen, a company of yeomen and two hundred ladies and gentlewomen on horseback. I was welcomed warmly and Mary was not there, so a great deal of tension went out of the visit. I played for hours at chess with my brother. We rode out together. I enjoyed watching him at tilting. He rode well and almost looked as if he were in training to be a knight. He put on evening revels and musical recitals for me. And, though it was still cold, we bundled up and took trips on the river on the royal barge. He took me to a muster of his men-at-arms on Blackheath, and we watched acrobats and high-wire artists. Edward loved them. We watched a play written for him by Nicholas Udall and we rode through London together, surrounded by his guards, yeomen, and knights. I went with him to inspect the naval dockyard at Portsmouth.

But by the end of the month, all the activities started taking their toll and he began looking pale and coughing again. I returned to Hatfield in hopes that he would quiet down in his activities.

Despite my precaution, at the beginning of April, right after I went home, I received a letter. Edward had fallen "sick to the measles and the smallpox."

Yet on the twenty-third of April he was well enough to

take part in the St. George's Day Celebrations at Westminster Abbey. He wrote to me, telling me how he had worn his heavy velvet Garter robes and that "this summer I intend to go on a royal Progress, to tour part of my kingdom, to meet my subjects, to be seen and to be entertained in the houses of the great nobles who live en route."

I had a feeling that I should see him before he left and so I made another trip, this time to Greenwich Palace, where the court was staying for the summer.

"I am thinking," Edward told me as we walked through the lovely knot gardens, "of changing the line of succession."

He looked feverish to me, and the spaces between his coughing fits were getting shorter and shorter.

"Why should you be thinking of succession now?" I asked lightly.

He bent to pat his new spaniel, who accompanied us. "Because I am ill, Elizabeth. Very ill. Only these noodle heads around me won't admit it. I summoned, in secret, the Italian doctor and astrologist Girolamo Cardano. I gave him permission, though it is against the law to cast the King's horoscope, to cast mine. He said he saw the omens of a great calamity. He told the council that all I need is rest, but he told me I have all the signs of consumption. And so I must think of who is to take my place.

"Someone," he finished, "has to be thinking around here. My council are all puppets. So I have decided to act. I can't have Mary be Queen. She is still Catholic. Can you imagine what that would do to England?"

I reached out to him, but he stepped away. "I'm thinking of naming Lady Jane Grey as Queen when I die."

He had another coughing spasm. It lasted long enough for me to turn cold and then collect myself. "Jane Grey?" I echoed.

"Yes. She visits me often. We are of the same mind about religion and in matters of state. She completely applauded my giving the priory of St. Thomas at Southwark as a hospital for the sick and my other acts of charity. She believes, as I do, that the council should be divided into committees. And, like me, she is all for continuing our father's policies, to name a few things."

*She is a fanatical Protestant,* I thought. *But yes, she will suit your purposes.*

"I have thought of you, Elizabeth, but consider it this way. Jane was supposed to be my wife. Sir Tom adopted her for that reason. We were just waiting until we got older. And you are so young and so innocent, I would not put this terrible burden on you. Not yet. What think you of my decision?"

What thought I? I thought that at least he should have asked me if I wanted to rule and let me decline. As if reading my thoughts he said, "Elizabeth, there would be open war in the land if I named you. I don't suppose for a minute that Mary could not raise an army against you."

He was right. Naming me before Mary would never do. "You have made a good choice, Edward," I said. "We are bound to obey you. You are King."

But I could not but wonder how much he had been influenced by Northumberland, Robin's father, who knew that if Mary took the Crown, all would be over for him.

In April of 1553 Roger Ascham returned from Europe. He rode the long road from London in his fine new cloak on a rainy day to see me. Cat Ashley ushered him in all in a flurry, offering him some sweet Tokay wine.

"My lady."

I was abed with one of my headaches, but Cat had dressed me quickly in a sea green bedgown as his arrival was announced. And opened the window to the warm, if drizzly, April day.

He came into the room and made his bow. He took off his hat and I saw that he now wore his hair shoulder length, that his boots were highly polished, his shirt the whitest, and his doublet of velvet. He who used to appear before me in a dusty black gown had learned much of dress in Europe.

"Roger, I've missed you."

"And I you, lady. But I fear for your health."

"Dr. Turner has declared it no more than one of my headaches brought on by womanly ailments."

"Ah, so you finally admit to being a woman—you, who I thought would never grow up."

"Sit, Roger."

He leaned over and kissed my hand, and then sat.

"Tell me about your travels. About the Council of Trent."

He sighed. "It was supposed to have been a league of

nations, sitting down to civilly discuss matters of religion and policy. A friendly discussion between Papists and Protestants, if such a thing could ever be. But they discussed everything else: the tumult in Africa, the organization of Europe into a solid front against the invading heathen Turk, the march of the German emperor into Austria. Religion became secondary."

"Have you visited court?"

"I have just come from there. William Cecil, the secretary, sends his regards."

Cecil, the young, Protestant, Cambridge-educated lawyer, who was a member of Parliament and had somehow taken it into his head to befriend me of late. I called him "my spy," for he frequently kept me apprised of what was going on in court when I wouldn't have known otherwise. Something told me I would need his services in the future.

"And my brother, Edward? Did you see him?"

"His condition is deteriorating. That is all I can say. It is against the law to . . ."

"Tell me."

He sighed. "He is becoming weaker as time passes. One of the royal physicians, Dr. George Owen, said he would be dead by June."

We fell silent for a moment. Outside the rain pattered. From somewhere in the house came the delicate music of one of my maids on the virginals.

"And what will you do now?" I said, giving the conversation a new turn.

"You no longer need tutoring, my lady, do you?" he asked.

"No. But I wouldn't be averse to you reading the classics with me every day and staying here. Now what else have you to tell me about court?"

"The Lord Protector, Northumberland, has betrothed Lady Jane Grey to his son Guilford, the youngest."

I nodded. "He wants to make his son King."

"There are those who say he uses his sons for his own ends. Well, he has five at his disposal." He glanced at me. "I am sure that Robin is beyond reach of his ambitious intentions."

"Go," I said. "I must rest."

Robin. What had he to do with his father these days? Surely his father needed him. Did he back Northumberland in all he did? Why didn't he write to me? Because he didn't want to involve me? Oh, Robin, when will I see you again?

Summer heat lay over the land like a wet blanket you could almost see. The corn was growing nicely, I'd been told, as were the wheat and barley and vegetables. But it was a terrible June and July for me.

I had just taken a powder for my head and some Jesuit bark for my slight fever when I heard a rider come galloping up to Hatfield. In a few moments I heard a commotion at the door and then steps on the stairway and down the hall.

Cat Ashley came in bearing a parchment for me. I took it, my heart thundering. Was Edward dead?

It was from Sir William Cecil, telling me that Northumberland was making a secret treaty with France, promising to give back Calais, the only land holdings England had there, in exchange for money and troops. "He has also," Cecil wrote, "forced London merchants to lend him fifty thousand pounds and sent armed forces to man the chief strongholds in the kingdom in case the people should rise in Mary's favor when Jane is named Queen."

I had instructions to destroy the note as soon as I read it. So I did.

On July third came another message from Cecil: The Duchess of Northumberland had visited Jane Grey, who was living at Chelsea, where Sir Tom had left her with his mother. She told Jane that when God called Edward to Him, it would be needful for her to go to the Tower, because Edward had made her heir to the realm.

The Tower was where all newly minted monarchs went just before their coronation.

Edward must surely be dying.

I forced myself out of bed. I called my maids to help me dress. I wore bright red in defiance of death, with an over-skirt of gold brocade. I had my maids do my hair and even put pearls in it. I went downstairs, weak but determined to be up and about when the news came.

I wondered about Mary. Were her spies sending her bulletins? Was she preparing to rise up against Jane Grey when Edward died? What army did she have, what ammunition and provisions?

I went out into the courtyard in front, blinking in the harsh midday sun. I sat in a chair under the shade of a large oak tree and immediately was attended upon by my maids, who brought me a tall, cold glass of lemonade and bade me keep out of the sun.

I saw the rider in the distance, in a cloud of dust like a mirage, coming closer and closer. Soon I saw that the horse was black and my heart skipped a beat. *Now,* I thought, *now, please God, don't let it be.*

My knights seized the reins of the horse as it clattered to a stop and the rider slipped down. He was wearing the green and white of my brother's court. He handed over another letter. This time it was from Northumberland.

They handed it to me and my eyes scanned the words *Edward* and *gravely ill* and *asking for you.*

Northumberland entreated me to come immediately to Greenwich Palace, in Kent, east of London, where Edward lay. I ran to the front door and into Cat Ashley's arms. "I must go," I said, "to the palace. Edward is asking for me."

That night, I had my maids and Cat Ashley make ready for a visit to the palace. I told my knights we would leave in the morning and they assembled the yeomen to make plans to travel.

We were in the courtyard the next morning, with the sun beating down to assure me it would be another blistering day. My yeomen were packing my luggage, my maids running in for last-minute things, when we saw another rider coming down the road.

As the rider approached, I saw that the horse was not black. It was the familiar dappled gray that had delivered its rider with messages from Sir William.

Breathless and sweating, the man drew up his horse. "Water," he said, "for me and the horse."

It was gotten. He gulped a full tankard of it then wiped his mouth.

"Give me the parchment," I ordered.

He wiped his mouth with his hand. "Princess Elizabeth, there is no parchment. The words are in my head and meant for your ears only."

I motioned for everyone to move away. When they did, the young man leaned toward me. "From Sir William. A warning. Northumberland wants to lure both you and your sister to London, where he will render you incapable of resistance. He may imprison you both. Or have you executed. Do not go. Stay here. Plead sickness. Mary is not going."

I reached out and touched his arm. "Thank you. Thank Sir William. I shall keep his messages a secret to my death."

The man nodded, and then mounted and slowly rode off.

More secret correspondence from Sir William told me that Edward died on July sixth at Greenwich. He died a horrible death, I was later told by those who were there. He had bedsores all over his body. He had a tumor on his lungs. He had a swollen stomach, and he vomited and coughed without ceasing.

A storm raged while he was dying. At Hatfield it seemed as if the heavens were coming down upon us, with hailstones making a horrible clattering noise, with lightning and thunder and wind.

Sir William told me later too that the doctors insisted on giving Edward a remedy they had put together for him. It consisted of nine teaspoonfuls of spearmint syrup, red fennel, liverwort, turnip, dates, raisins, mace, celery, and pork from a nine-day-old sow. "God deliver us from physicians," Sir William said.

Dr. Owen and Sir Thomas Wroth attended him when he died. His valet, Christopher Salmon, was there, and his close friend Henry Sidney held his body as he died.

The storm raged on all night. I scarce slept. But I knew somehow that this was no ordinary storm. There are those who say they saw my father pacing about on the battlements of Greenwich Palace as it raged, and as Edward died.

## CHAPTER THIRTEEN

*J*ust outside the front courtyard of Hatfield was a tree, a huge silvery maple with a hole in the trunk. When we were children, Robin and I used to leave notes for each other in the hole, and Sir William Cecil's messenger had sent word via a letter that I should check the tree trunk at least once a week, because there might be a message there besides the ones delivered by his man.

With all the events leading up to Edward's death I had forgotten to check. After Edward died, I went to the tree, and sure enough, there was a folded bit of parchment with a letter from Sir William. It was dated the thirtieth of May. I had missed it.

It told how Jane Grey was wed to Guilford Dudley on the twenty-first of May. There were six white-robed bridesmaids. The wedding took place in the Dudley private chapel. The bride wore a gown of gold embroidery and wore her hair in braids. My brother had been too sick to go, but had sent costly jewels and gold plate. The festivities took place at Suffolk Place and then Jane was escorted back to Chelsea Manor, and Guilford went to his own home.

Northumberland was taking no chances. He did not want the marriage consummated yet, lest things change. Then it could always be annulled.

Only later did I wonder how Sir William knew about the tree trunk. And with a reassuring warmth of my spirit I realized that Robin had told him.

Right after Edward died, a rider came garbed in all the finery of the court, with two knights guarding him. There was a letter from Northumberland.

It was borne by Sir Nicholas Throckmorton, a court official based at Greenwich. I invited him and his knights in for refreshment.

He gave me the letter. It was a bribe from Northumberland. He would, he wrote, give me several properties that Edward held, including a new town house and the castles of Woodstock and Pontefract, plus promise of a queenly allowance every year if I would give up my claim to the throne.

I went into my study to answer the letter. Woodstock! It was a dilapidated, ancient royal manor, far off in Oxfordshire where one could go if one expected to die.

Pontefract! Scene of the murder of Richard II in 1400!

"You must first make this agreement with my elder sister," I wrote back, "during whose lifetime I have no claim or title to resign."

Sir Nicholas departed, leaving behind him standards for Queen Jane and demanding we fly them from the front tower of Hatfield. But I intended to do no such thing.

So there I was at Hatfield, daily reading the classics with Roger Ascham and riding and practicing archery, hearing nothing and daily checking the tree trunk and trying not to look down the road for messengers.

There were other ways of learning the news. Travelers stopped by on their way from London, and my knights went to tilting tournaments, invited by noblemen in the area. I was invited too, but I declined. I did not want to leave Hatfield. My knights came back with gossip, which I learned to separate from real news.

"On the seventh of July the Tower was reinforced," they told me.

"On the eighth of July the city was informed of the King's death. On the tenth, Jane was brought to the Tower and proclaimed Queen."

Still I refused to fly her standards from the tower of Hatfield, though Cat Ashley urged me to. Then I found another letter in the tree trunk from Sir William that informed us that Mary was staging a revolt. Robin Dudley, under orders from his father, had ridden with men to Hunsdon, her palace, to arrest her, only to find that she had fled northeast to Kenninghall in the heart of her East Anglian principality. Men were flocking to her standard.

She had landlords of her estates, neighboring lords and gentlemen, as well as Catholic officials with her. She had scores of common people.

Another letter was left in the trunk: On the eleventh Mary proclaimed herself Queen.

Then the messages stopped again. Oh, I was at my wits' end. So my sister was raising an army and would fight. Then a couple of knights who were riding in the area stopped by. Over wine, meat pies, and vanilla wafers, they gave us the news.

Jane was not happy as Queen. When they told her of the honor, she answered, "The Crown is not my right, and pleaseth me not. The Lady Mary is the rightful heir."

London was quiet. There was no rum piped into the streets, there were no bonfires or fireworks or celebrations of any kind. No lyrical poems were written. The people did not want Jane. They wanted a Tudor, not a Grey.

I stayed quietly at Hatfield, sending out no letters, no replies to letters, and no ladies-in-waiting on errands, except to the apothecary. Of course they came home full of news. By the twelfth of July, so many followers had arrived at Kenninghall and pledged themselves to Mary that she had to move them all to Framlingham, a commodious brick lodging built by the Duke of Norfolk in the twelfth century.

It had thirteen great towers and a mighty wall, forty feet long and four feet thick.

I would have done the same thing, I decided. I was fascinated by my sister's moves. She, elderly and alone, was acting like a King. *Yes,* I told myself, *yes, there is something in us Tudors.* I knew that I had the body of a woman, but I had the heart and stomach of a King. But I had never suspected the same of Mary.

I followed her actions with great interest and grasped at scraps of information.

Sir William wrote again: "Robert Dudley was routed at King's Lynn and forced to retreat to Bury St. Edmunds to wait for reinforcements."

As it turned out, I did not have to wait for letters from Sir William Cecil anymore. People came up to Hatfield's gates with news to give to me. My knights and yeomen were busy keeping them at bay.

Mary had fifteen thousand men and the number kept increasing. The council wanted Jane Grey's father to ride out with an army to East Anglia, but Jane, for once acting the Queen, said no, Northumberland should go, not her father. Northumberland was the best in the kingdom. So he left, promising her, "I will do what within me lies."

But soon Mary was proclaimed Queen in Cheshire and in Devon. Even Robert Dudley, knowing he could not do as his father wanted, proclaimed her Queen.

Four more counties proclaimed her. In the Tower, Jane's noblemen were leaving, her ladies-in-waiting were making excuses and parting from her also. Her treasurer had absconded with money.

One morning Richard Vernon brought me a placard that had been nailed to Hatfield's front gate. It announced that Mary had been proclaimed everywhere but in London.

Mary now had thirty thousand troops. Northumberland's men, realizing that to stay with him meant treason and death if Mary won, were deserting him in droves. He was left with a skeleton crew in the field, so he himself declared for Mary.

On the nineteenth she was proclaimed in London. "Queen of England, France, and Ireland, and all dominions, as the sister of the late King Edward VI and daughter unto the noble King Henry VIII."

Now the city celebrated. Bonfires were lit up and down the streets, and rum flowed like water. Caps were thrown in the air and money was thrown out of windows. Trumpets blared, there was shouting and crying from the people, and bells pealed from all the churches. The city fathers gave orders that "fountains and conduits were to run with wine."

I feared for Robin. Would he be put in the Tower because of his father?

"Worry about Jane," Cat Ashley told me. "She's a slip of a girl at the beck and call of greedy, evil men. Now all have deserted her. What will she do?"

Indeed. We found out later that Jane's father burst into the royal apartments in the Tower and tore her canopy and told her she was no longer Queen. That she must lead a quiet life. Jane was happy, we learned. She wanted to go home. But her father said no, and she was locked in her royal apartments with whatever attendants were left while her husband, Guilford, went to the White Tower to be with his mother.

He was like a baby duck, I was told. Always paddling after his mother. Jane had to be beaten twice by her parents before she would agree to wed him.

Soon guards were placed at the doors of the Tower. Jane was prisoner.

The sound of bells ringing all through the countryside came to us on the wind. Bells for Mary. They went on night and day for two days. Cat Ashley insisted we have a feast of celebration. "You never know what spies are about," she whispered to me, "and so we will celebrate for Mary."

I did not need further encouragement, and so a feast was planned. We invited our neighbors, the families of nobles, and knights and had feasting and dancing enough to give lie to anybody who said I did not support Mary.

Then came a letter from my sister. The parchment had a red Tudor rose stamped on it, and though her script was not as good as mine, at least she had written it herself.

"I send my greeting to my most beloved sister and bid you ride with me into London to give thanks for my deliverance and yours."

"It's a summons," Cat told me. "Nothing less."

"Which I dare not ignore," I answered her.

I made ready to go to and greet Mary. The letter said we were to meet at Wanstead, to the east of Waltham Forest. But I would ride to London first, and establish myself at Somerset House, which I owned.

On the twenty-ninth of July I left Hatfield with two hundred horsemen armed with spears and bows. Everyone wore the green and white of the Tudor clan. I rode through Fleet Street to make a grand show of it.

Once I had established myself inside Somerset House, Richard Vernon asked to see me.

"Lady," he said as he bowed, "I have a concern."

"Tell me."

"I think you should not ride to Wanstead with all these men. It could be mistaken as a show of force to your sister, the Queen."

The sense of it struck me. Why had I not thought of it? What kind of a Queen would I make? I must think more clearly. "Thank you, Richard. Your opinion means much to me. You are right, of course. Tomorrow morning we ride out with only you and my other knights and a few yeomen."

"I'm not thinking clearly," I told Cat Ashley. "What would I do without the advice of my knights?"

"It is why you have knights," she told me.

"But when I am Queen . . ."

"You will still have them. And other advisers."

I noticed she no longer scolded me for saying what I would or would not do as Queen.

"I need Sir William Cecil," I said.

"You are doing fine. Trust yourself."

"Do you think Mary will take me prisoner? Do you think she will make me become Catholic? I heard that Robin is in the Tower. Do you think she will have him put to death?"

"You ask questions that none of us can answer. Only this can I give you. Your knights would die for you before they allowed you to be taken prisoner. The people would revolt. She cannot make you Catholic in your heart, where it matters. And remember, your friend Robin proclaimed for her in the field."

Oh, what would I do without these good people around me? I did not want to ask.

The next morning, with my knights and a handful of yeomen and ladies, we set out for Wanstead. I wore one of my old gray velvets, the only splash of color being the ruby cross at my neck. I wore white trimmings and allowed myself a circlet of pearls around my head, but around my waist I wore only a prayer book encased in silver filigree.

Outside Mary's palace of Wanstead, crowds of people milled about, sat on the grounds, even walked in the garden. My knights cleared the way for me to walk through. Inside, the great house was overpowering and echoing. Our steps sounded on the polished marble floors. Paintings and tapestries dwarfed us. Scribes and messengers were scurrying in and out, as were servants carrying huge platters of wine and fresh fruit, cheese, and bread.

Mary was holding court.

"Make way for Elizabeth, sister of the Queen, here at the Queen's command."

Out of the corner of my eye I saw them all, those gentlemen who now felt as comfortable in Mary's court as they had in Jane's and Edward's. Who could always change their loyalties as they changed white shirts and velvet doublets. There were the Earls of Bedford, Winchester, and Pembroke, all the senior lords from the privy council, Lord Shrewsbury, Sir Nicholas Throckmorton, Lord Clinton, Sir William Pickering. Even my kinsman Lord Howard was there. The Howards were the most powerful Catholic family in the kingdom. My mother had been part Howard. Catherine Howard had been married to my father before he had her beheaded. And, sure enough, there were Sir James Croft and the Earl of Derby. I recognized them all from my brother's court.

And there at a desk in a far corner was my friend Sir William Cecil, Secretary of State.

All eyes were upon me as I was announced and went to kneel at Mary's feet. "Your most holy Catholic Majesty," I said, "I thank God for your deliverance."

"And I for yours." She got up, stepped forward, and raised me up. She kissed me. Her kiss was cold, her sentiments shallow, I perceived. The whole court was watching. What could she do?

To my amazement she was dressed in red satin trimmed with gold. She wore diamonds and pearls, rubies and gold. How did we look together, I wondered, I in my plain gray, set off by my flaming red hair, and she in red satin that made her look pale and sickly? Did people notice?

My time at Wanstead was like a dream. And the next day we rode for London. Together. I rode just behind her in the parade, followed by my knights and yeomen. All along the way people came out and cheered, waved banners, threw flowers, offered fruits and sweets, shouted blessings.

Mary wore ceremonial clothing, a gown of purple velvet and satin in the French style, covered with gold and gems. She wore a chain of gold, pearls, and precious stones around her neck and a French hood trimmed with pearls. Her horse was white and proud, caparisoned in cloth of gold with embroidery. I dressed in white, plain as could be, trimmed only with pearls. Behind me rode Anne of Cleves, my father's fourth wife, whom he had put aside because he "liked her not." She was a sweet lady, always glad to be included in ceremonies, never jealous of any new Queen.

I waved and pretended the rejoicing was for me. Mary shouted, "Pray to the Lord." And I thought, *She doesn't know how to be a Queen. She doesn't know how to accept the adulation of the people. Humility will get her nowhere.*

We rode straight for the Tower of London. Outside its gates hundreds of children dressed in white sang for her and threw flowers. Cannon sounded, echoing off the water of the Thames. The sound of it gave me courage.

For a few minutes, before we reached the Tower, I dared to ride abreast of her. "Madam, I would inquire of you. Where are the Dudleys?"

"In the Beauchamp Tower, to stay there and await their fate."

"And my lord Robin?"

"With the others."

"He was not part of the scheme against you."

"He fought with his father," she said. "He rode against me both at Norfolk and at King's Lynn. He came to Hunsdon to arrest me."

"But, Madam, he declared for you in the field."

"Enough about Robin Dudley. Now get back to your place in line."

I had provoked her. She came quick to anger. I must be careful.

But I could not help worrying about Robin.

I could not keep my eyes off Beauchamp Tower as we approached. Was Robin, at that moment, looking out one of those small windows at us?

At once, Sir John Gaze, the Lord Lieutenant of the Tower, came out to greet Mary. He bowed. She sent one of her knights forward and he was handed a paper. The Lord Lieutenant read it, bowed again, and said, "Your orders will be immediately complied with, Your Majesty."

Then he went into a part of the Tower that held more prisoners, and soon we heard a clanking of chains and a shuffling of feet.

Never did I see such disreputable-looking humans as those who emerged from the inside of that Tower. Their clothes were bedraggled and some still had chains hanging from their wrists. Their hair was over-long, their faces haggard.

I did not know them all, but I recognized the Duchess of Somerset, the widow of Edward Seymour, who had been beheaded two years ago. Another I recognized as the Bishop of Winchester, imprisoned for God knows what. And they told me that the third one was Edward Courtenay, son of the Marquis of Exeter, who had been beheaded fifteen years ago. *So this is young Edward,* I said to myself. In spite of his ragged appearance, he was very manly and handsome.

They all knelt at my sister's feet. She ordered them released, and I thought, *Well, at least some good has come out of her being Queen after all.*

"And where is Lady Jane?" I asked.

As we turned to go, my sister sniffed. "In Traitor's Jail, where she belongs, while I figure out what to do with her. Isn't Edward Courtenay handsome? Did you see him look at me?"

I was startled. I had not. Did she imagine it or just want it? I was taken aback by this display of girlish coquetry by my much older, severe sister. Was she looking to marry? Of course! It came to me only then. She must wed and have an heir. It was not only the duty of a Queen. It was something she had to do if she wanted to keep me from the throne.

And only now would she bury our poor brother, whose body was sealed in a lead-lined coffin. She would have him buried with full Catholic rites and have me kneel in the Queen's chapel while it went on.

The council warned her not to do it. All of London would protest, they told her, at the idea of a Catholic Mass in Westminster Abbey. But she went ahead and did it anyway. And I thought, *Oh, Edward, how you would rise up at the chanting of the monks, the sputtering of candles, the acrid smell of the incense, and the whole mystifying Roman affair. This would have killed you if nothing else did.*

I stayed at Greenwich Palace for a brutally hot August. My second week there, I had a visitor, Sir William Cecil.

"Lady, I wanted to tell you that I have resigned my position as Secretary of State. I wish to retire to my homes in Wimbledon and Burleigh. But my concerns are for you. How will you fare?"

"I wish you were not leaving. I have come to depend on you."

"I can no longer live as a spy," he said. "I would not last two minutes with Mary. But I wish you always to consider me your friend."

"I need friends," I told him.

He nodded. "Princess, beware. The French and Spanish would like to see a return of England to the Church of Rome. The French and Spanish ambassadors would be happier if you were not . . . around anymore. The court is full of enemies. Be careful to whom you speak and how. Don't, under any circumstances, let Mary force you to become Catholic. The people do not want a return to Rome. They look to you to save them from such a fate. The hopes, desires, and hearts of the people rest with you. They look to you now in this time of danger. And that puts you in harm's way. Be wary. I know you can survive."

Then he knelt at my feet and kissed my hand, and I felt like a Queen already. The peoples's hopes, desires, and hearts rested with me! I understood what he was saying. And I was sorry to see him go.


In Spain they had the Inquisition, I knew, in which thousands were burned alive if they were suspected of not belonging to the Catholic faith. Soon everyone in the palace was bandying it about that Mary would marry either young Edward Courtenay or Philip, the Prince of Spain.

Marry the Prince of Spain! And bring into dear old England fear, Spaniards, cruel priests, and burnings! The people would be in an uproar. They would, I felt sure, never stand for it.

Rumors were rampant. They flowed like the wine through the conduits in the streets. Mary had written to Pope Julius II in Rome, promising him the return of England to the Church. She never went about but that Edward Courtenay, whom she had decided to befriend, was at her side. Yet she was in negotiation with Prince Philip of Spain for marriage.

She summoned me to her. I went, expecting the worst. "You have declined to go to Mass," she accused me. "I wish you to study the Catholic faith and to attend Mass daily."

"Madam, I am not worthy," I said. I had prepared all my answers ahead of time.

"God decides who is worthy, not you. He will welcome you."

Her coronation saved me. Readying for it, she seemed to forget her command. We took barges to arrive at the stairs of Westminster Palace. The sun was bright, the water gleamed, and on it were all barges decorated with flags and ribbons, with musicians inside serenading the Queen.

As Lord High Chancellor of the realm, Stephen Gardiner performed the coronation. It was long and yet exciting. *Someday,* I thought, *someday, all this will be for me.* Afterward we went back to Westminster Hall for a banquet. I expected to be snubbed—at the very least to be consigned to a lesser place than I warranted—but I was not. I was put in a place of honor at the table as the Queen's sister. Next to me sat Anne of Cleves, who at one point put her hand over mine and in her still-heavy German accent said, "Be brave, child. But don't be foolish. The difference between the two is as nothing."

That was all she would say. Somehow it cheered me.


When Parliament was called now for the first time in Mary's reign, Gardiner made the announcement that Catherine of Aragon's marriage to my father was legal. My father's world-renowned divorce from her was to be forgotten, and so his marriage to my mother, Anne Boleyn, was, without Gardiner's saying it, illegal. Thus I was illegitimate.

After the coronation, the court moved to Whitehall, and Mary summoned me again. "Well? Are you going to go to Mass?"

It was September. Outside, the world was blue and green, gold and red, ablaze with celebration of the harvest and the wealth of the kingdom. Fields were busy with peasants cutting and stacking. The smell of wheat permeated the air. It was so good to be alive. I wanted to go home to Hatfield, but I dared not ask permission.

"Madam, I have been sickly. I have had the greensickness and bilious fever."

"I do not believe you. I wish you to come to Mass with me this Sunday. It is the thirteenth after Trinity, the Feast of the Nativity of the Blessed Virgin Mother. It is a holy day for us both. It is God's day for virgins. If you do not come, if you anger me, I cannot promise what will befall you. Only, let me say this: Countess Margaret of Lennox comes every Sunday. She brings Henry Darnley with her. He is now a long-legged twelve-year-old. Who knows but that, if I do not have a child, he might have claim to the throne? After all, he has our father's Tudor blood."

Back in my apartments, I wailed, "Cat, what will I do? This Sunday is my birthday. I'll be twenty years old."

"Remember what I once said: God knows what is in your heart. No one can dictate that. And remember too, you want to live to be twenty-one. And do not let talk of Henry Darnley upset you. She will use any threat, but the boy can never be your rival, for all his having Tudor blood."

I did not have to pretend sickness that Sunday. I awoke with one of my headaches. I had to be coaxed to eat, to dress. No powder was needed to make my face pale, and I had to be nearly dragged to Mass by Cat Ashley and Lady Browne, one of my attendants.

I went, near to fainting. And, to my surprise, who came into the chapel but Countess Margaret of Lennox with young Henry Darnley.

She smiled at me, and put her hand on her son's head. No words were needed to convey her superiority and confidence.

Mary was so happy about my "conversion" that she sent me a diamond-and-ruby brooch and a rosary made out of coral.

But, to ensure that I would not escape from Whitehall and go home, she kept me locked in my lodgings. The only time she let me out was for an audience with her. And those came about every other day. I was summoned to kneel at her feet and to answer for my lack of progress in studying the Catholic faith.

"Do you not believe in the sacraments?" she asked me.

"I believe what every good Protestant believes."

"Why don't you wear the rosary beads I gave you?"

"I am afraid I might lose them."

"Don't worry. I have more."

So I wore the coral beads at every audience I had with her. And in every audience she threatened imprisonment. It was there, in the sound of her voice, in little things she said.

"How does it look for the sister of the Queen not to attend daily Mass?"

"I don't think anyone is really looking," I said insolently.

"Do you not hope to make me happy in my old age?"

"I hardly think you old yet, Your Majesty."

Always, I was dismissed in anger, with veiled threats and enough rancor to make me feel the little sister who had put a toad into her bed.

And from those around me, even Pussy Cat: "You must placate the Queen!"

"You must return to the Old Faith!"

"She is depending on you to act as a true sister!"

"What will the Spanish Prince say when she weds him and her sister is a Protestant!"

My head spun with these remarks. My sleep was no sleep at all, but nightmares.

On the verge of illness, I took Cat's advice. "Go to Mass. Pray to God in your heart. He knows what is there. Everything else is an outward show."

Once I did, Mary backed off. She raised my place in court, she gave me gifts, she let me accompany her when she rode out, which was seldom. "I would ride more," she explained, "but Courtenay is not good on a horse."

She still kept Courtenay with her, Prince Philip or no Prince Philip. I was twenty, she was thirty-seven, but I felt old.

As September progressed the news was all bad. Jane Grey was still in the Tower. The Spanish ambassador was pushing my sister to sign an order for her execution.

Northumberland was beheaded, though the other Dudley men were not. Not yet. I prayed for Robin. But there was some good news. After proclaiming her mother's marriage to my father legal, Parliament refused to do anything else that Mary wanted.

They were afraid of rumors of her impending marriage to the Prince of Spain.

## CHAPTER FOURTEEN

*M*ary and I struggled for weeks, sparring with each other over my lack of attendance at Mass. One minute we were friends, the next enemies. I pretended, constantly, that I was sick, but in spite of an attack of headache, she still insisted I go. I must get back to Hatfield, I decided. Word would get around that the Queen's sister was converting, and all those people in the streets would have no one to look to as Queen in the future.

Still we argued, and Mary considered no blow too low. "Are you even my half sister?" she demanded loudly one day. "Some say that Mark Smeaton was your father. Remember, he was a lover of Anne Boleyn."

Mark Smeaton, a musician, had been executed for having a love affair with my mother. Of course Mary would bring my mother into it. The stain on me from her would never go away.

"Then you might as well say I'm a witch, as they say she was!" I shouted back at her.

"All Protestants are witches," she finished.

Were we both weary of it all? Finally, as the fall deepened, I came down with the ague, and a terrible wracking cough. Perhaps, remembering that cough in Edward, she consented to let me return to Hatfield for the winter. To rest.

That winter I felt beaten, lost, and dejected. So did my people: Cat Ashley, Mr. Parry, and all my knights and yeomen. I kept a quiet house that Christmas, although we did have a feast. I wanted no word to get back to Mary that I was enjoying myself. I read the Greek Testament with Roger Ascham, who had kept busy in my absence writing a book on his travels.

In early December Mary got the council to approve her marriage with Prince Philip of Spain. How?

"The council is composed of the elite," Roger Ascham explained to me. "The elite have no fear of a foreign marriage. The ordinary people do."

In court, if you so much as listen to a secret plot you are connected to it. I knew that, after growing up as daughter and sister to the reigning monarchs, but I could not very well have had Sir James Croft silenced when he told me of the new uprising, could I?

He came, uninvited, one day to Hatfield. He was a courtier who had served my brother. "Princess, I have news."

News was precious to me. "Yes?"

"Your sister is to wed Prince Philip of Spain."

"We all saw that coming."

"England will be a subject of Spain. And of the Pope. She must be stopped."

I felt the beginnings of a plot. "What will be will be," I said.

He lowered his voice. "Sir Thomas Wyatt is planning a revolt."

Sir Thomas Wyatt. I knew of him. His father had loved my mother. The son had made his name by being successful in many military operations.

"What will be will be," I said again. "I want no knowledge of it."

Croft could be a spy, sent to implicate me. Or he could be with Wyatt, wanting my support. Either way I was in trouble.

"I want nothing to do with this," I told him. "I want to know no more."

But I did want to know more. I was starving for news. I sent my trusted knight John Chertsey out to sniff around and find what he could. He was a master of disguise and dressed himself as an ordinary citizen. He even changed his voice somehow.

He came back the last week in December.

"The rebellion is to take place on Palm Sunday, Princess, the day the Prince of Spain and all his people are to arrive in London. Its primary purpose is to put down the Prince and prevent the marriage. They know it is a sacred day and no one will be working and the roads will be clear. They intend to march on London."

"How many men do they have?"

"Some four thousand."

"And the leaders?"

"Besides Wyatt there is Lord Henry Grey, father of Jane, who still hopes to see his daughter on the throne, and Edward Courtenay, who feels angry at your sister for putting him aside and planning to wed Prince Philip. There are others. . . ."

"Do you think they have a chance?"

"Princess," he predicted, "this is December. By March the whole plot will have leaked out. It did not take much for me to find out about it."

As it turned out, he was right. The last plot to overthrow Mary failed miserably. Jane was not crowned Queen, and instead she was further incriminated. On February eighth the latest grim news to me came by Chertsey, who had again gone abroad to scout.

"The plot failed, Princess. Wyatt mustered his forces at Kent. The Queen sent the Duke of Norfolk out against them."

"But he's eighty years old," I protested.

Chertsey shrugged. "He had a detachment of the guard and five hundred city whitecoats. Wyatt had split his men. He came to Southwark, at the southern end of London Bridge, to find the drawbridge up and guarded with cannon. He fled to Ludgate, but was finally taken and is now in the Tower along with the other rebels."

"Thank you, John. Is there something else?"

"Yes. The Queen rode out at battle's end to see the dead bodies, the men screaming and blood all over the place. Astride her horse she heard someone say, "This will happen again and again as long as Lady Jane Grey lives.""

He looked as if there was more. "And?" I asked.

He was hesitant, but I nodded my head and he told me. "The plan of Wyatt was to overthrow the Queen and put you on the throne, after they had married you to Courtenay. Now they speak of you as if you had a hand in the plot. It has endangered you, my lady. As badly as it has endangered Lady Jane."

Never before had I truly felt that my life was in danger. Now I did. If Mary thought I had helped plan to overcome her government, my head would not long be on my shoulders. I went to bed that night and waited to hear the hoofbeats of soldiers approaching Hatfield. Near dawn I fell asleep. They came when I had been asleep only about an hour.

I heard the thundering of horses' hooves when they were still miles from Hatfield. They came just as dawn was breaking, a hundred horsemen strong in velvet coats, and a hundred more in scarlet cloth trimmed with velvet. All were armed. They carried my sister's standard. To take one Princess, apparently, was the job of a herd.

I was still in my robes when they came into the house— my great-uncle Lord William Howard, Sir Edward Hastings, and Sir Thomas Cornwallis.

With them were Dr. Owen and Dr. Thomas Wendy, both of whom had attended my brother, Edward, when he died.

"I can't go. I'm sick. Look at me!" Even as I spoke my arms, chest, and face were breaking out in a red measles-like rash. I drew up my sleeve to show them my blotched arm, but the doctors only ushered me upstairs to examine me. Cat stood by nervously.

They blamed my reddened skin on "nervous energy," and insisted I was well enough to travel. If I could not ride a horse, I would be taken in a litter.

I dressed in white. They put me in a litter and carried me. I was carried through Smithfield and along Fleet Street to Whitehall.

The Queen refused to see me.

I was lodged that night in the shabbiest of Whitehall's chambers. I could not eat, I could not sleep. I could only cry, to Pussy Cat's dismay.

Then Chertsey, my head knight, came to my quarters, to tell me that Lady Jane and her husband, Guilford Dudley, had died that very day I was taken, beheaded for their part in the plot. Her father was soon to be beheaded.

Though I had never liked her, my heart broke. She was

only sixteen! How young to die! Had she gone to the block quietly? Or was she hysterical?

"I'll wager she scarce knew of the plot," I told Chertsey. Just as I knew nothing of it. Would I too lose my head?

The council questioned me for days. They came constantly to my chamber and set themselves up as paragons of loyalty to Mary and tried to get me to confess I'd been part of the plot. I had been allowed only two ladies with me besides Cat; two gentlemen, Mr. Parry and John Chertsey; and four servants. Guards were placed outside my door. They asked the others to leave when they questioned me.

Bishop Gardiner and Lords Arundel and Paget did the questioning. They tried six ways at once to name me guilty at the onset.

I dodged their questions like a squirrel dodging stones thrown by a small boy. Bishop Gardiner was the worst. "You are Her Majesty's main target for refusing to return to the Old Faith. What will she tell her new husband when her own sister refuses to embrace it?"

I knew that the outcome, for me, would be life or death, that any day they might come in and say I was condemned to the block. For I could not prove I had not been part of the plot.

"You weren't in communication with Sir Thomas Wyatt?" they asked.

"No."

"Do you deny that Sir James Croft came to you and told you of the plot?"

"I knew nothing about a plot. If told, I would not have wanted to know."

"Sir Thomas Wyatt has accused you of being a strong backer of the plot. Do you deny this?"

"I never met Sir Thomas Wyatt except for seeing him in court. You must have tortured him to get him to say this."

How I held up I will never know. But I met them eye to eye. I never looked away or faltered. I did not let my voice waver. It was strong and clear and at all times the voice of a future Queen.

And then, toward the end of the third week, it happened. Gardiner himself came to tell me that the Queen had given him orders.

"You are to be taken to the Tower," he said in that cold, grating voice of his. "Make ready to be moved."

As a final act of vehemence, Mary took away all my people except Pussy Cat and two maids.

"This way, my lady."

The council led me to an ominous-looking barge at the pier. You went to the Tower by water. So many had, and never returned. I shivered all the way in the light rain of a dreary March day. And even though my Pussy Cat held my hand, it didn't help. I was terrified.

And then there was the Tower, nightmare of every Londoner's dreams, replacing hell as the ultimate seat of punishment. And there was the Traitor's Gate, through which all prisoners were led to climb the slimy steps and go up through dark archways that smelled of waste and con- taminated water, of death and despair.

They were waiting for me: a dozen yeomen of the Tower with the Lord Lieutenant, as they must wait at the gates of hell for the worst sinners to enter.

"I can't go in there," I sobbed.

"You must, my lady." The voice was kind, as was the touch, helping me out of the barge. Who belonged to that voice I did not know, but I did know that if I lived and some- day became Queen, I would find out and reward the man tenfold.

I had to step in the filthy cold water that lapped over the bottom steps. Someone else put out a hand to help me. A few of the wardens and workers came out and looked at me from the top of the stairs. Then, as if someone had given a signal, they all knelt and called out, "God save Your Grace!"

Somehow that gave me the courage I needed to climb the slippery steps to Traitor's Gate.

"I am innocent of charges brought against me," I said. "I am no traitor. I cannot go through there."

The Lieutenant of the Tower put out his hand. "Come, Your Grace," he said gently.

"When they send me to the Tower Green I will have a sword from France sent to do the job on my neck," I told them, "like my mother did. I will not have a clumsy English axe."

Somehow, with the help of the Lieutenant of the Tower,

I got to the top and went through Traitor's Gate. They put me in the Bell Tower, the tower next to Robin. How odd to find the playmate of my childhood alongside me in this place of depravity and death!

They took away Cat Ashley, which caused that good woman to burst into tears, and I had to comfort her instead of her comforting me. They took away my ladies too, and gave me Isabella Markham, who was married to Sir John Harington, and another lady by the name of Elizabeth Sand. Both were very pretty and yet not shallow. Both attended to me with kindness and respect, which was a great comfort.

From my window I could see the scaffold. I could watch, if I wished, as Jane's father and uncle were beheaded. I did not wish to watch.

Outside the cold walls the March wind whistled and betimes turned into gales. At night the wind moaned for all those who had spent years in this terrible place. When the sun came in during daytime, it only seemed to create shadows. The walls ran with dripping water. The halls echoed footsteps and the calls of the guards, and at night I could hear moans and betimes screams of the other prisoners.

So I passed my days as a prisoner. Daytime, I read my *Book of Common Prayer* or sewed or embroidered, or talked with my ladies. Meals were not bad. My table was set with the proper silver and plate and goblets, and somehow I suspected that what was being put before me was far better fare than the ordinary prisoner got.

The days went on. How had Courtenay lived in here

since he was a boy of twelve? How had Lady Jane done it for months, all the while seeing her own death coming?

The doctors visited me and said I was in good health except that I needed some fresh air and sun. Dr. Owen said he would ask Sir John Gaze, Lord Lieutenant of the Tower, if I could walk outside a bit every day.

March became April. The rushes on the floor of my lodging began to stink. And every day when one of the Queen's men came to bait me, I thought he was bringing a warrant for my death.

Mary did not kill Courtenay. She spared him because of his royal blood. And that gave me hope.

And then one day, the Lord Lieutenant of the Tower came into my chamber. My heart near stopped as he knelt before me. "News, your ladyship. Yesterday Sir Thomas Wyatt was executed. And before he died he admitted that you and Courtenay had naught to do with the plot. Thanks be to God."

My ladies talked with the guards and so the word came to me. After they executed Thomas Wyatt his body was cut up and put in a basket in a cart and brought to Newgate, where parts of it were hung all over. His head was parboiled to preserve it and placed on top of the gibbet at St. James. But somebody stole it away within a week.

They told me that when the people of London heard I was pronounced not guilty, they celebrated in the streets. They lit bonfires and demanded my release. They drank toasts to "the young red-haired Bess."

Because I was proven not guilty, I was allowed outside to smell the blessed fresh air, to walk on the battlements, to hear birds overhead. It was still April. The world had come alive. Though I was still a prisoner, my heart was restored.

In my first week of such unheard-of freedom I was allowed to walk in the garden. Spring flowers were all in bloom and had never looked so lovely to me. I gazed at the azaleas and irises and lilacs and daffodils as if I had never seen such before. Children were playing nearby and I was told by a guard that they were the children of the jailers. They lived here. *What a place to bring up children,* I thought. The guard smiled at me. "They are happy," he said, as if reading my thoughts.

All the guards I passed smiled at me and gave bows and answered my questions. They called me "Your Grace."

One day as I was walking in the garden a small boy came up to me. In his hand he held a bouquet of flowers.

"For my ladyship," he said, with a little bob of his knee.

"Why, thank you, child. Where did you get them?"

"From the woods and water meadows nearby. The gentleman had me give them to you."

"What gentleman?"

"Up there." He gestured with his head to Beauchamp Tower. "Says these ones in the middle be ragged robins, and I should point them out to you."

Tears came to my eyes. "Thank you, child. Tell the gentleman I thank him."

## CHAPTER FIFTEEN

*F*lowers from my Robin! Was he, even at this moment, looking down on me? I looked up at the small windows of Beauchamp Tower. Was there someone in the window? Was he waving, or was it my imagination? Just in case, I waved back and then I smelled the flowers. A beautiful nosegay, come from my Robin, whom I hadn't seen now in how many years?

Did he know what I'd been through, what I had suffered? But what of *his* suffering? He was under the sentence of death for his part in helping put Lady Jane on the throne in the first place. He and his father and brothers were still in prison, not knowing if each day was to be their last.

I must get a note to him. Would the boy come tomorrow?

Would I get the Lieutenant of the Tower, good man that he was, in trouble, by passing a note? Should I ask his permission? No, for that way I would get the little boy in trouble too. I had learned from another guard that the child was just five, that his name was Henry Martin, and that he was the son of the Keeper of the Queen's Robes in the Tower.

No, I could not get the little fellow in trouble. Could I send my Robin something? No to that as well. Too many good people would be hurt, perhaps even Robin himself.

I went back to my lodgings, which had been aired and sweetened in my absence. I showed the flowers to my ladies, who oohed and aahed over them as if they had come from the Queen's knot garden.

But out of my own window I could see that the scaffold had not been dismantled yet. Were they not finished with their work, then?

The next day I walked out again, and again the boy came, this time with a bouquet of forget-me-nots. "The one man in Beauchamp, he gives me coins every day, and I get up early in the morning and pick them from Fenchurch fields."

I clutched them to my breast. "What is the man's name?"

"Lord Robert Dudley. He says to tell you he is still your faithful Robin."

"Tell the man I thank him, that I think of him," I said.

The boy nodded and ran off. *Oh, Robin.*

The next day Henry Martin told me that "the man's

wife did come. But all she did was cry. He doesn't give her flowers."

*Oh, Robin.*

It went on that way, every day that week. And then, on the eighth day of my walk, as I was being escorted back to my lodgings by a guard and we passed a low brick wall, I saw eight black ravens line up on top of it. I knew they would not fly away, that their wings had been clipped so they could not fly, in keeping with an old legend that when the ravens left the Tower, it would fall.

They stood stock-still, eyeing me with their beady eyes as I passed. All eight of them. One for every day of my walk.

That night the Lord Lieutenant of the Tower did not visit me as he usually did when the day was done to see if I needed anything.

That night came instead a man who walked like a soldier, who was clad all in black like a priest, and who gave only the slightest of bows as he came into my apartments.

"Madam, I am Sir Henry Bedingfield. I have orders. You are to pack your things and get ready to depart this place tomorrow."

The words were so frightening to me that I could see them hanging in the air between us, echoing as if in a tunnel. "For what reason?" I asked.

"It is not given to you to know. I have my orders. I will be by at the crack of dawn tomorrow to see you out. But you should know that the Queen has banished Edward

Courtenay from the kingdom."

I felt ready to faint and after he left had to sit down. My ladies brought me water and smelling salts. "They are going to kill me tomorrow," I said.

"No, Your Grace," both assured me. "He did not say that. And didn't he say Her Majesty pardoned Edward Courtenay?"

"Yes, but banishment. Where will he live abroad? Banishment from England can be as bad as death. Will she banish me?"

But I knew somehow that it would be death for me and I scarce slept that night. I thought about Sir Henry Bedingfield. As I could recollect from my history, his grandfather had entertained my grandfather at Oxburgh Hall, near Swaffom. His grandfather had fought beside my grandfather in victory at the Battle of Stoke in 1487. His father had been the jailer for Catherine of Aragon, Mary's mother. Now he had become my jailer and I could only imagine Mary's satisfaction. When I did fall asleep, it was only to have screaming nightmares about Mary's mother being jailed and sick and dying at Kimbolton, and my father refusing to let the child, Mary, see her mother before she died.

Now I knew why I sometimes heard screams in this place at night. And now, this night, others could hear mine.

I was up early, insisted on being dressed in white, and started giving away my jewelry to my ladies. I could not eat breakfast, and I looked in vain for the Lord Lieutenant of the Tower, but he did not come.

Instead Sir Henry Bedingfield came with a dozen armed men, some the Queen's own Guard. They took up positions outside my lodgings, at the gates of the Tower, along the paths. So, I thought, this is the way it is to be.

As I stumbled out into the misty morning, I heard the echo of seagulls over the river, smelled its dampness, and could not help but notice that the eight ravens *were still lined up on that stone wall, looking at me as I was led away.* Surely that was a sign, but of what? And speaking of signs, was I not to be allowed spiritual counseling?

Then I near stumbled on my way to Tower Green and the scaffold, and was assisted by two soldiers. But we were not on our way to the scaffold! We were walking down to the riverfront; that was why the gulls and the smell seemed to permeate the air.

"But this isn't the way to . . ." My voice faltered.

"To a barge on the river, Your Grace," came Sir Henry Bedingfield's voice, a little kinder now. "You are going on a journey."

"No! Not to the wharves. Not on a ship," I pleaded. "I do not want to leave England!"

"Woodstock is in England, lady. You are under house arrest. You are a prisoner of the state."

Oh! I felt happiness. I was not to be banished from England!

The River Thames was smooth and shining on the twentieth of May, the day I was helped into the barge to go upstream again. And though it was early of the morning and no one was yet up and about, as our barge passed the Steelyard, home of the wealthy Hansa merchants, cannon boomed halfway through our journey, echoing off the water.

Cannon. A salute for me. Would Mary curse them, hoping the town would not know I was being released? Someone had disobeyed any orders she had given to keep my departure secret. It made my spirits soar.

Woodstock was my destination, but that was five days away. We continued on upstream until we reached Richmond, a dozen miles away. Sir Henry Bedingfield—my jailer now, but a kind and decent man—told his men to tie up at the pier of Richmond. In the distance I saw the strange outline of turrets and domes: Richmond Palace, which my grandfather had had built.

We stayed the night. As we were ferried across the Thames the next morning, I saw a group of my knights and ladies standing on the bank waving to me. I got Sir Henry's permission to write them a note.

It was from the Bible: *"Behold, I send you forth as sheep in the midst of wolves; be ye therefore wise as serpents and harmless as doves."*

As we traveled through the countryside that day, the people came out of their houses and threw flowers and came up to me with sweetmeats and cider. "God bless the Princess!" was the constant cry.

Sir Henry did not like it. He sensed discontent with the Queen. So we pushed on and he would not even let me stop to thank them.

The next night we stayed at the dean's lodgings at Windsor. I was constantly under guard.

The rules were simple, Sir Henry told me. "You are to be kept under guard, but treated as may be agreeable to Queen Mary's honor, state, and degree. You are to have no conversation with any suspicious person outside of my hearing. Neither are you to send or receive any message, letter, or token to or from any manner of person."

We spent the next night at Sir William Dormer's house at Buckinghamshire, and the next at Lord Williams of Thame's Rycote at Oxfordshire.

And everywhere we went, people were waiting on the shore for me: scholars from Eton, men, knights, and women with more flowers and cakes and wafers.

They crowded me; they said, "God bless you, Bess." They cheered, they rang church bells, and Sir Henry had all he and his men could do to keep the peace.

Then we had to travel through the villages of Oxfordshire. In every one, Wheatley, Stanton St. John, Islip, and Gosford, people turned out to celebrate me, to cheer.

Finally we arrived at Woodstock, in the outlands of Oxfordshire, the ancient royal estate where kings had hunted for centuries. The place rose out of the woods like a haunted castle, with missing slates on the roof and broken windows gaping in the shadows. It was a near ruin.

It had a huge outer courtyard and an inner one not much smaller. And Sir Henry liked it because it had only three doors to be locked.

There was no mention of the open windows through which one could try to escape. But where would one go?

The outbuildings were a ramshackle mess. The gardens were overgrown and the bushes needed pruning. Weeds grew up in the brick walks. Neglected flowers bloomed sadly, with no one, until now, to see them.

I learned what banishment felt like. It was almost worse than the Tower. There was no Robin here, though I hadn't seen him in the Tower. There was no Henry Martin to bring me flowers. I even missed the ravens that had lined up to stare at me.

I knew what these old, rundown castles in the outlands stood for. They were places where one went to die, places where prisoners were put to grow old in exile, to be forgotten. My fate was worse than that of Anne of Cleves, the wife my father had rejected. At least she was still allowed to come to court, to be a part of things.

And in banishment I stayed for ten months, near kept under lock and key, without my Pussy Cat, who'd been taken from me. A week after my arrival my knights had come to help guard me from harm. I was allowed only three maids.

But the people of the countryside knew I was there.

One day I was summoned downstairs by Bedingfield. "A young man is here to see you."

*Robin?* My heart leaped. But no, I didn't know this young man.

He bowed. "John Fortescue, your ladyship. A student at Oxford."

Oxford was only five miles down the road.

He brought three books for me. But, because it was discovered that he was a stepson to Mr. Parry, the books had to be sent to London to be examined by the council.

They were approved and came back, to my delight.

So Sir Henry didn't want me to converse with suspicious persons? Yet next came another young man, named Christopher Edmonds, bearing fish and two dead pheasant cocks.

Bedingfield checked his background to find that he was the stepson of Lord Williams of Thame. We ate and enjoyed the fish and the pheasant.

Then came one Francis Verney, a son of a rich and influential Buckingham-shire family, bringing a lapdog.

Sir Henry was driven near daft by the visitors. Who was smuggling me messages? Who was whispering plots to get me out of here?

I felt sorry for the man. He was not mean or demeaning. He tried to be kind without being friendly. He had his orders to follow, and would follow them to the death. But he could not take my measure. Soon I and my knights and ladies laughed rings around him.

The best sport we had was with Mr. Parry. Mary wanted him away from me, but Sir Henry did not want responsibility for the bills. And those were to be paid by me, I soon was told. I was to pay Sir Henry, my jailer, and his staff and the household help. The council paid only his soldiers.

Sir Henry realized we needed Mr. Parry to pay the bills, so he had Parry housed at the Bull Inn in the town of Woodstock. Soon the Bull Inn was making all kinds of money on visitors and those who came to stay a day or two.

My people. Bringing messages. And from Woodstock my faithful servants found reasons daily to visit Mr. Parry, and he, in turn, sent me news of events I would otherwise not know about.

And so I learned of Mary's marriage to Prince Philip of Spain. They married at Holy Cross in Winchester. I was glad not to see Mary play the dewy-eyed bride, because she was near forty and with graying hair and I could not think of her as such.

Would she have children with him? If she did, my turn in the succession would be ruined. Yet, could I pray she didn't? Mayhap what Mary needed was a child to devote herself to.

Mr. Parry's complicated group of informers told him all about the wedding. First the groom, then the bride, walked from the west doors of Holy Cross to the steps of the sanctuary. Mary was given away by four nobles. Her wedding ring was a plain gold band. And according to an ancient rite, she promised to be "bonny and buxom at bed and at board."

After the wedding ceremony, they traveled through the countryside, hunting and dancing. At Windsor, Mary had Prince Philip installed as a Knight of the Garter. She herself placed the collar around her husband's neck.

*Well, let her be happy,* I thought. *She has waited long enough. As long as she doesn't allow him power as King of England.*

And then I worried about Robin. Would she take it into her head to execute him? Oh, how I prayed for Robin!

*Well,* I thought, *if I'm going to pay the bills, I'm going to live in decent lodgings.* And so I had Sir Henry hire gardeners to set the outside in order; painters to redo my chamber, my sitting room, and the kitchen and dining hall; men to repair the roof and the broken windows of Woodstock. Soon Sir Henry, who could not complain because it was my money, was following my orders.

My people had even more reason to visit Mr. Parry at the Bull Inn. He had to approve all expenditures and pay the bills.

"You are setting up your own court and kingdom, Princess," Richard Vernon remarked to me one day.

And the thought struck me full face. I *was,* even in exile. Was this what pretenders to the throne did, then?

In the fall my people came back from the Bull Inn one day to give me the news that Mary was going to have a baby and the midwives said it would be a boy. And in the fall came the news that Robin still lived.

"Bess!"

"Pussy Cat!"

We embraced on the front steps of Woodstock as she

alighted from the carriage. It had been ten long months since we'd seen each other and now we both shed tears.

"I wrote dozens of letters to the Queen, asking her to let me come to you," she said in a tearful voice as her head rested on my shoulder. "And now that I'm here, I'm almost jealous that you got on so well without me."

"You old Ash-Cat."

"I'm starved. Do you have something to eat?"

"Of course, you old dear. Do you think I starve just because you're not around?"

We spent the winter undisturbed at Woodstock. There even came a rhythm to the days, with me riding out with my knights or staying indoors and reading Greek and Latin and attending Mass every day to keep Mary happy. We had music and good food and I almost forgot the worries of the outside world until Sir Henry received a letter one March day bidding me return to court.

"Why?" I asked.

"To attend your sister at her lying-in. And because Prince Philip thinks it about time he met his dear sister Elizabeth."

The letter came to Bedingfield on April 17. And just like that, we were given orders to pack up and head back to London. My imprisonment, though I was still guarded, was over in a second. *What was it all for?* I asked myself.

And then I told myself, *This is what you can do if you are*

Queen. Imprison a person in the Tower or at Woodstock as befits your whim, and then set her free in the blink of an eye. It is called power, fool, and you will have it one day.

We arrived at Hampton Court on the twenty-ninth of April, at dusk, and we entered privately on the garden side to the Prince of Wales's Lodging, where I was given a suite of rooms for myself and my people. Sir Henry showed me the secret access my suite had to the royal apartments.

The next morning we awoke to bells ringing and anthems being sung throughout the palace, and the news that the Queen was delivered of a son.

But by that afternoon the rumor was afloat that the news was false.

"There is no child," Pussy Cat whispered to me.

"What do you mean, no child?"

"No baby was born. The information was false. She was not pregnant."

"What was it, then?" I was dumbfounded.

"Nobody knows. Except mayhap her desire to bring forth a child. Don't question it. For your own safety, don't ask a thing when you see her."

But I was not summoned to see my sister until two weeks later. And that summons came late at night and we did not take the secret access to her apartments. Her men came to my door, with torchlights in hand, to take me outside and across the garden to the foot of the privy stairs that led to her bedchamber. The torchlights cast fearful shadows. The bushes, sculpted in the shapes of animals, came alive.

Instead of the fragrance of flowers, I smelled the stench of death.

I had taken the time to dress in my best, my white satin decorated with small pearls. As it swished when I walked, I thought they were taking me outside to assassinate me, about how my blood would look spilled on the white gown.

I must always be in fear of death. For if Mary had no child, no heir, was I not next in line for the throne? And where would that leave her husband, Philip?

As I knelt at Mary's feet I could not help but notice how old she'd gotten, how pale she was, how lined her face, how sickly her look. No robust motherhood here, I thought.

"You have not yet converted," she accused me, "to the true faith."

"I have been attending Mass at Woodstock, Your Majesty."

"How can I trust you when you refuse to cooperate?"

"I am your sister."

Her laugh was sharp. "My husband insists we be friends. But I cannot help but keep you under constant guard. You represent a threat to me. What would you have me do?"

"As Your Majesty thinks best," I said humbly. For just then, behind her throne I saw a curtain move and I knew without being told that someone was there, listening. But who?

Was her husband that underhanded?

"My first pregnancy proved false," she said to me. "But I will bear a child. You will not succeed to the throne. I will yet bear a child!"

"I am sure you will," I told her.

Prince Philip stepped out from behind the curtain then, a man of small stature yet large presence. He was perfectly groomed and looked at me with sorrowful brown eyes as he held out his hands. "My dear sister," he said, "welcome back into the family circle."

I had Philip with me, though I knew not why. Had Mary complained of me so much that he grew tired of hearing it? Was he truly sympathetic to the abused younger sister, or did he just fear that if she died in childbirth I would be in line for the throne?

Dear God, did he think that if Mary died he could marry me and become King? The thought made me draw upon all my strengths. I must be careful around this man. I must always think of tactics and attacks and regrouping my strengths, as if I were at war.

In the months that followed, although I was kept under watch and not allowed to roam freely, my life improved. I became part of the court and Philip paid constant mind to me. He danced with me, he flirted with me, he defended me against Mary's tirades.

I must say that in some of her extravagance, my sister surprised me. Even I, who remembered my father's court, was stunned to learn what my sister spent a year on her table, and that eighteen kitchens were kept going at all times. In order to feed all the Spanish ambassadors; Philip's knights, soldiers, and servants; all Mary's ladies and aides and servants as well as the council; and visiting dignitaries, she went through in one day eighty to a hundred head of mutton, a dozen of fat beef, a dozen and a half of veal, poultry, game, deer, boar, and rabbit.

But what stunned me more than that was that every time I sat with them at table, Mary ate from gold plates. Philip ate from silver.

Was she doing this to let him know he would never be King? I did not know my sister's mind. Betimes I thought she was more mad than my father had ever been.


By Christmas, Mary declared she was with child again. And the whole charade began all over.

One morning, the week before Christmas, I was in the knot garden, for it was a fair, beautiful day. I looked up to see a slow, black smoke drifting up over Fleet Street. Fire?

I ran inside to tell Cat. But she knew it wasn't just any fire.

"It's your sister's work," she whispered.

"What work?"

"She's burning people she says are heretics. She started yesterday. She says she must cleanse England. Why do you think, when I finally reached you at Woodstock, I urged you to hear Mass? There was rumor this was coming. Only now"— and Cat's voice broke—"now she must make amends and make sacrifices so her child will be born alive. There will be many burnings from here on, Bess, so just be quiet about it."

Burning people? It could not be. I did not keep quiet. I

went to Philip. "Is it true, my lord, that the smoke out there is from executions?"

He nodded silently. "It must be. The true faith must be restored. Your sister has decreed it."

"But people are being burned alive."

He shrugged. And then I remembered that in Spain, under the Inquisition, they did this all the time. And I was in a state of fear for myself and for Robin. True, I had gone to Mass at Woodstock and here. But what would happen if she put it to me to convert to the "true faith" or be burned? Would I have the courage to be burned, as those poor souls in London had?

She made no excuses for what she did and she meted out no mercy. Rich and poor were burned, male and female, sometimes even children. Just for not being Catholic. She burned popular preachers, artisans, farmers. Some were blind or lame or could not hear. One woman was with child. Mary would, she vowed, cleanse England.

Sometimes I wished my sister dead. Was that a sin?

Philip was leaving! He broke the news to Mary. He had suffered a terrible disappointment when there was no child. How could he be a true English monarch without an heir?

So, I thought, both King and Queen feel unfulfilled when there is no child. Well, since I shall have no King to disappoint, I will bear no child.

He was going back to Spain to attend to business. His father, Charles V, had decided to abdicate and leave the throne to his son. Philip told Mary not to worry. He would return in a few weeks.

Mary was frantic, tearful and half mad with worry.

"You won't be here when the new Prince of Wales is born," she cried.

"I will be back. I promise," he said.

My serving ladies told me that Mary tried to hold on to Philip in those last few days before he left. She tried to convince him of her stature, her state in life, her Queenship.

They went in a procession through London. At Tower Wharf they took royal barges to Greenwich.

They went to the Observant Friary, which Mary had refurbished. Our father had thrown out the monks after he broke with Rome and was seizing and closing down monasteries. Mary brought them back. She and Philip prayed, and on their return to Greenwich hundreds of people bearing torches accompanied them and stayed outside the palace while they said their good-byes. Then Philip, heir to Spain, the Low Countries, Austria, Sicily, Naples, parts of Germany, and the Americas, whose wife would not allow him to eat from a gold plate, left for Dover and the ship that would take him home.

## CHAPTER SIXTEEN

*M*ary continued being sickly after there was no child, or to put it in her words "no Prince for the kingdom." She stayed in her chamber, praying. She went to Mass twice a day. And I am ashamed to say that I went with her. For outward appearance I had converted to Catholicism. I hoped the people and God would forgive me this charade. I knew many others who had "converted" to avoid being burned at the stake too.

Mary wrote to Philip daily in French, signing herself "your humble and obedient wife."

Nature was in keeping with my mood. In September of that year, the year I was twenty-two, heavy rains came to England. The rains brought deep flooding, and people and animals lost their lives. Crops were ruined.

Mary made me fast for three days. "You must atone for your sins," she said, so I fasted her Catholic fast, for which I would receive an indulgence from the Pope.

Then things got worse. Philip started answering Mary's letters with the demand that he soon be crowned King of England. Mary said she had to ask the council and Parliament, who had to approve first.

Philip wrote that he would not return until he was made King.

Then rumors came to England that Philip was enjoying himself in the Netherlands, that he daily went on hunts and attended weddings or other festivities wearing a mask. That he romped with his male friends until the early hours of the morning.

That he was having an affair with Madame D'Aler, a beauty of whom he was enamored.

Mary got thinner and sicker. She almost stopped eating, but she went on. She ordered more burnings. Even Oxford Archbishop Cranmer was burned at the stake.

Philip wrote again, asking that all his people be sent back to him, his clerks and household help, and his confessor, Alfonso de Castro.

Now the public attended the executions, not to watch, but to demonstrate their anger, to raise an outcry.

It was whispered that many longed for the Queen to die and be succeeded by her sister, Elizabeth. This only placed me in more danger, so I assured Mary of my loyalty.

Mary had her cooks bake Philip's favorite meat pies and

shipped them to him.

Philip wrote, "My honor will only allow me to return to England if I am allowed to share the government with you."

My old friend Sir William Cecil wrote to me, "The French are getting ready to march on Spain. It is said that Philip asks Mary for money for the war and she is pouring money into it. She is selling, borrowing, and making us bankrupt here at home. Just to get her husband back."

His word was true. My allowance was cut in half. Mary gave no explanations.

Now there were uprisings, some serious and some put down immediately. Sir Henry Dudley, a distant relation of Robin's, was raising a force to land on the Isle of Wight and march on London. The plot was discovered and put down. People were questioned, tortured, put in the Tower, and hanged. Mary tried, by having my apartments searched, to connect me to the plot, but she could not.

To apologize, she gave me a diamond ring for my birthday.

People were secretly sending me presents to prove their loyalty to me. Sir Nicholas Throckmorton sent me a pair of perfumed gloves. Lord Paulet of the privy council sent a necklace of pearls that had once belonged to his mother. Lords Clinton, Derby, Bedford, Pembroke, Sussex—all on the privy council—sent bottles of scented water, velvet slippers, gold-trimmed neckerchiefs, and boxes of sweet-meats. All "for my birthday," which was September 7. But I understood. The nobles were declaring their loyalty to me.

Somehow, Philip contrived to return. He said, laughingly, that his father was afraid of angering the Queen of England, who has so graciously supplied Spain with gold and silver, arms, and provisions for her army.

So, Philip returned—fresh from the "mating dens" of Amsterdam, it was flung about. He returned in February of 1556.

Philip wanted me to marry.

Oh, it isn't as if the subject had never been spoken of before. Over the years there had been many negotiations for my hand, some even serious. But I never paid mind to them because that was part of being a Princess of the realm. By the time both parties were ready to honor such negotiations, their countries might have been at war, or at the very least at odds, and so all promises were broken.

But now was different.

Now King Philip was my brother-in-law. Now my "intended" was his son from his first marriage to a young Portugese woman, who had died in childbirth. His name was Don Carlos. And he was all of ten years old.

Philip returned to England with the joy of it on his lips and in his face.

"I have told Carlos all about you, Elizabeth, and he is truly smitten," he said on the day they broke the news to me.

"But he's only ten years old!" I cried. "By the time he is

old enough to wed, I'll be an old lady!"

"It is your duty to wed as you are assigned to wed," Philip reminded me. But I knew he only wanted me to marry his son so that if Mary died the boy would be King of England. And England would still be under the thumb of Rome and the Catholics.

I refused. "I will not! I will never marry anyone!"

"Not marry?" Philip laughed at me. "It is your bounden duty! Now go and write to Carlos and tell him how happy he has made you by his offer."

I knew, of course, that it was one more of the dangers of being a Princess, to have an arranged marriage. Yet I was determined never to marry, by arrangement or not.

But the dangers of that winter were numerous, and not only mine.

War came, war with France, a country better equipped than ours. And we were losing. Mary soon was with child again and all groaned and prepared for a new ordeal. She grew in girth. And the more battles Philip lost, the more she burned people at the stake in London.

I stayed away from her. I managed, somehow, to wrangle her consent to go back to Hatfield.

Hatfield, my childhood home. There were my people ready to greet me, Mr. Parry and Roger Ascham among them. Hatfield, where I could speak without being afraid, where I did not have to worry about what mood Mary would be in today.

Where I did not have to watch my every utterance to

Philip. Or hear the rumors that he had gone abroad in London last evening to seek out women. Or that he liked poor and parentless little girls.

I settled in at Hatfield. I hunted with my knights, I checked the larders, I even greeted people at the back door who came with corn and flour and vegetables from the gardens of my estates. One thing was different about these farmers this year, however.

They all knelt before me. They all called me "Princess," and their eyes shone when they spoke to me. They told me about the fall rains and floods and how they had managed to save the wheat just in time. And how many animals they had lost. I encouraged them to talk, and soon they were telling me how they waited for me to become Queen.

I shushed them good-naturedly. And then they would ask about Mary's new baby, and take off their hats and promise prayers for the little one.

Letters kept coming to me from Don Carlos.

"My love," he wrote, "I cannot wait until the day we meet. My father has told me of your handsome looks, your skill at sports and at hunting. The whole of my life lies in the balance until I see you with my own eyes. Wait for me."

I ripped up the letters and threw them in the fire.

Somehow word got out through London that Don Carlos was wooing me. And the people began to riot. They did not want this son of a Spaniard for their King. Weren't the burnings enough to keep Mary satisfied?

And then, one day, came a letter with a different hand-writing, but one I instantly recognized.

"My dearest lady," it read.

*It has come to my attention that they want you to wed*
*Don Carlos, son of Prince Philip. My lady, I have*
*intelligence which should put you off from such a plan.*
*The young man in question suffers from insanity.*
*He is deformed, not only in body, but in mind. He has his*
*people haunt the brothels and bring home women,*
*whom he then has whipped and tortured. He loves to*
*torture horses and rabbits and cats. He has plotted*
*to murder his own father and take his Crown. My lady,*
*refuse to do this terrible thing and tell your sister*
*your reasons. She may be cruel, but not cruel enough to*
*bring such a malcontent to you and to England.*

*As you know, I have been released from the Tower*
*but consigned to Framlingham at Norfolk, and*
*look forward to the day I may again serve you.*

                                        *Robin Dudley*

Once again my Robin had saved me. I would go to my death rather than marry this Don Carlos. I would tell Mary what I had learned.

But I didn't. I didn't have to. Mary was told by her advisers that to send me to Spain to be married would anger the people. She would have riots. And so the matter was dropped.

I heard later, from one of my knights who had been to London for a jousting tournament, that Mary had consulted many people about sending me to Spain. That she "conceived that by removing Elizabeth bodily from hence, there will be riddance of all the causes of scandal and disturbances."

But everyone told her that to send me away would be the cause of insurrections.

There were other requests for my hand: Emmanuel Philibert, the Duke of Savoy—Catholic and soldier— asked. The King of Sweden asked on behalf of his son.

Somehow I managed to wiggle out of any engagement. *Somehow*, I thought. Had they heard of Mary's pregnancy? Were they asking for my hand as Queen? I would not marry, I told Mary and Philip. I would not marry anyone.

## CHAPTER SEVENTEEN

It was raining hard one day at Hatfield, a chilling autumn rain, when Cat Ashley came to me. "Princess, we have found a woman at the back door with two little children clinging to her."

I was not surprised. People, hungry people, had been coming to Hatfield and the surrounding estates all fall, begging for food, some near death's door. "Is she dead?" I asked.

"No, Princess, but near to it. She has not eaten anything except some wild weeds and nuts for a week now. The children are . . ."

"This is terrible, Cat."

"Yes, Princess."

"I have no recollection of England ever being in such a

state. I hold my country in great affection but am ashamed now. In this last year more than sixty people were burned at the stake. There are uprisings all over. Poverty and sickness are rampant. The people are discontented. The coffers are empty because of the war. The Queen is poor. There is war with France, who, I'll wager, will take Calais back before long. We have no friends abroad."

I looked around and then back at my dear friend. "What is to be done, Cat?"

"Princess, we can only wait. There are plenty of good men about, doing just that, waiting."

I sighed. "Have the woman and her children fed," I said.

I came and went, back and forth between court and Hatfield. I was no longer a prisoner but was under guard, and I doubt I could have gone far without Mary's men apprehending me. Moreover, I could not leave Hatfield without the Queen's permission. The more I matured, the more I resented the way my sister, the Queen, treated me in her reign. No, she had not had me beheaded. But was I to be grateful for that? The people would not have stood for it. The people were my hope, as I was theirs.

To show my goodwill and loyalty to my sister, I made some baby garments, a little organdy dress embroidered all over, little underthings, and bonnets. My sister held them close and her eyes shone. "Oh, for the little Prince," she said.

Then she showed me the nursery. There was a cradle

made of golden wood and carved with Latin and English verses. A cloud of a skirt enveloped it. There was a counterpane of blue silk trimmed with lace. There was the bed she would deliver the Prince in, covered with the lightest of cotton sheets, all trimmed with lace, and there were wrapping cloths for the child, and shawls and booties.

My heart constricted. She spoke so often of the little Prince that he began to take shape in my imagination. And in some bizarre moments I even cried for him—for I, as well as others, was sure he did not even exist.

People came and went at Hatfield all the time. We were constantly welcoming them, constantly feeding and entertaining them.

One day Robin came riding up as if he had never left me, accompanied by some knights and yeomen. I did not know him at first. I thought he was some nobleman I had not met. He was tall and broad, manly and dashing. Never had I seen such a handsome specimen of man since Sir Thomas Seymour.

"Princess." He fell to his knees.

"Get up, Robin," I chided. I brought him into the house and we hugged, though his sword got in the way and the medallion around his neck and the metal buttons on his surcoat bit into me.

"Why have you come, Robin? Is there some danger I don't know about?"

"To see you, Princess. To tell you that I have sold some

of my estates so I might bring you gold for any need that may come to you in the future."

"Robin! My old friend. No one has any gold these days."

"My men have it for you. You have only to ask Mr. Parry where he wants it. And there is more. Those close to you are planning in case you have to fight for the throne. Sir William Cecil and your own Parry have been in touch with Sir Thomas Markham, commander of the garrison at Berwick against the Scots. Markham has been canvassing about and has secured a force of ten thousand men in case you have to fight."

"Robin, you could be declared a traitor for this."

He smiled. "I was declared one once. And I am only too glad to be one again, if it means helping you. Once again I declare my support. You have only to ask."

Another man came to Hatfield, this one not so welcome.

It was the Count de Feria, Philip's Spanish ambassador. He was sallow of face, seeming always to be plotting. He was arrogant and had always looked down on me. But that was before. I sensed my growing importance in the country and was not about to be looked at down anybody's nose, especially not his.

We took dinner. Alone. I sent my servers from the room. I sensed he had something important to say. And he did.

"Prince Philip sends his regards," he said. "He hopes being here at Hatfield isn't distasteful to you."

"I could never feel distaste for my own home."

He bowed his head in a nod. "One of many you own, I understand. You are a woman of property, are you not?"

"I am a Princess," I reminded him.

He spooned his soup noisily into his mouth. It dripped from his beard. "You would still be at Woodstock if not for Philip. He convinced your sister to let you come to court, did he not?"

"He did."

"Otherwise you would not be sitting on so high a horse now, Princess. You owe Philip much. He is convincing your sister to name you as heir in her will. Does that not please you?"

I bit my lip to hold my temper. "My father named me in the line of succession," I said. "It is my rightful place. Mary is not giving me anything."

"Ah, but she is monarch. She could change those directions, as your brother, Edward, changed them when he was King, naming Jane Grey Queen."

"I believe the people of England will be heard from on the matter."

He cut his meat. "They say if you were Queen, you would favor Sir William Cecil, Sir Nicholas Throckmorton, Sir Peter Carew, John Harington, Lord Robert Dudley." He smiled. "Poor choices. All Protestants. Some exiles, some plotters, some condemned traitors. Dudley is an outlaw, a wanton."

"He is a good man, and whom I favor is my business," I told him.

He nodded. "Giovanni Michieli, the Venetian ambassador, said you are a vain and haughty person, like your father. I say you are a clever woman, thoroughly schooled in the manner in which your father conducted his affairs."

"I respect and admire my father's policies, yes. And am fortunate enough to be well schooled in them. As I am in his father's policies."

He leaned back in his chair and sighed. "You are not to be bested, I see. I think you need a husband, ladyship. You should have wed Don Carlos."

I could scarce keep from laughing. "I heard his father kept him tied to a mummified corpse, night and day for two years. No wonder he is mad. But even were he not, the people would never abide my being out of the country. That is why I would not consider the offer of the Duke of Savoy. I saw how my sister has lost the affection of the people for marrying a foreigner. I think you and my sister and Philip know that."

The dinner was finished. He bowed when he left. And I felt just a little taller.

## CHAPTER EIGHTEEN

*R*eports came to me at Hatfield almost daily, about Mary. I was determined not to be frightened by their ominous tidings, nor to fear for my sister, though I was convinced she was mad.

But then came a report that Mary had awakened from sleep one day and told her attendants, "I was surrounded by little children, singing and playing, like angels."

I decided that she was my sister, after all—in spite of all—and I would go and help attend her in her illness.

It was the middle of October 1558 when I set out for St. James's Palace in London, where Mary had taken up residence. I had just turned twenty-five in September. The previous January Calais had fallen to the French, a great loss. This fall, influenza swept through the land, killing thousands. It was rumored that my sister suffered from fevers and had been brought back from the brink of death by a Dr. Cesar. Next I heard that she was discussing Parliament's agenda with her councillors.

I had learned much in spite of all my travails. I had learned one lesson in humility more important than all the others: You are only as good as those surrounding you, whether you are a farmer or next in line for the throne. Mary had not had good advisers. Everyone tried to take from her, including her husband. I, on the other hand, had always been surrounded by good people, from Cat Ashley and Mr. Parry to Robin and Sir William Cecil and Roger Ascham.

Another lesson I learned: When you are Queen, it is never a good idea to share power, which meant, in my mind, that I should never marry.

When a Queen is expecting, she spends a month locked in her chamber with none but her chosen ladies at her side. Mary was locked in her chamber, but not for that reason. She had locked herself in, I soon learned, alone. She thought everyone was out to betray her. She trusted no one.

Philip was still abroad. She cried for him daily, they told me.

They told her I had come to see her, and so she opened the door and let me in. She looked as if she were having a child, all right. She bulged in front, but she told me the baby didn't move and she was afraid it was already dead.

Her child was due on November 1, she said. On

October 31, she insisted on getting up from her lounge and showing herself at the window to the crowd below, from a side view, so they could see her bulk and cheer the child that was to come.

On November 1 a choir went about the halls of St. James's singing the Te Deum in honor of the baby to come.

But no baby came.

And nobody made mention to Mary of the fact that it would soon be a twelve-month babe. I stayed in the chamber with her as much as I could, in spite of her ramblings and weepings, her paranoia about people who wanted to kill her, her crying for Philip. She would not eat any of the food brought to her.

"They are trying to poison me," she whispered.

Her hair hung about her, unwashed. She was clad only in a nightdress and robe. She did not look at all the Queen. I felt ashamed for her and tried to comb her hair, to suggest that she dress.

"Leave me be," she snapped, "or I shall throw you out with the rest of them!"

I should not have, but I poured her some hot mulled wine and offered it to her. She slapped the goblet from my hand and it clattered onto the floor, leaving a red stain. "Elizabeth, you are excused," she told me.

"I will serve you. Someone must."

"Go!" She pushed me from the room. And when I turned back I saw she had collapsed in tears on the floor. "I have lost

Calais," she said, sobbing. "That was to be my legacy as Queen. And I have not even a child to leave them."

I set myself up outside her door. Midwives and servants and doctors came and went, only to be screamed at and thrown out. One minute the palace echoed with her screams, the next there would be dead silence in the echoing halls, and the next, the far-below sounds of the Te Deum being chanted and sung.

"If they don't cease that hymn I'll go mad," I told my knight John Chertsey, who had come to see if I wanted anything.

"Tell us and in a minute we'll be ready to go, Princess," he said quietly.

I looked into his dear face. It had the lines of maturity now and I warmed at the thought that he and my other knights had always been there for me, like older brothers.

"Thank you, John, not yet," I told him.

As I sat there people came and went, asking me if I wanted or needed anything, if I wouldn't rather retire to my chamber and rest, or wouldn't I like some fruit or cheese?

Many of the maids and courtiers who came to inquire of me or ask after Mary knelt before me. I felt uneasy, then thought, *They know it is just a matter of days before you are Queen.* And so I acted accordingly, raising them up and telling them the lady they should kneel to was inside her chamber. Nobody was fooled by this charade, but I felt it necessary to act it out anyway.

The door suddenly opened and Mary stood there. "I have

need of some armor and a sword. They took all my fighting materials away from me. Go and fetch some."

"Madam?" I asked.

"You heard me. I want some armor and a sword. Now!"

John Chertsey fetched them for me and offered to bring them inside. I declined the offer and brought them in myself, struggling with the armor. John placed himself outside the door and whispered that I should cry out if I felt I was in danger.

She accepted the armor and sword like a gift. "Go now."

"Madam, I would stay with you."

"I say go!"

I was tired of being insulted, of being treated like a lowly servant, but I bit my lip and told myself again that she was my sister and how long could she last now?

I went out the door and pressed my ear against it. All was silent for a while. Then I heard the scraping sound of the sword being lifted from its scabbard and I glanced at John and tried to open the door. But it was bolted.

At once John put his shoulder against it and smashed it in. At once Mary's knights came running and of a sudden we all stood in her chamber, gaping at her.

She stood, hoisting the sword, the armor clumsily drawn across her swollen middle. "I will protect Calais to the death!" she said. "To my death and that of my child."

Immediately her ladies and knights rushed her and wrestled the armor and sword away. "Madam," they cried. "Madam, there is no need for this!"

She fell to her knees then and cowered in a corner, crying. "What's to become of the kingdom? I'm dying!"

"No, you're not," I lied.

"Then what is this thing inside me? Certainly it is not a babe."

"I'll stay with you," I promised. "I'll stay."

We got her settled. They gave her some wine with opium in it. And I thought, if there is a babe, that will kill it. But I could do no more. I must have looked terrible, haggard and distraught, for my other knights and James and Richard Vernon were in the hall with me of a sudden, and John Chertsey was giving them orders to make ready, to get our people, that we were going back to Hatfield.

I protested, but John only looked at me. "Princess, forgive me for disobeying you, but she is dying. When she dies, you will be Queen. You must think of your duties, your obligations, your kingdom. You can do that back at Hatfield, not here where you are treated like a court jester."

His language was strong but he was right. I got permission from the council and we went back to Hatfield.

Before I left, I saw Sir William Cecil and Sir Nicholas Throckmorton and told them to let me know right away when my sister died. They were only too glad to agree, and promised to keep me informed about everything.

It was November 5 when we arrived back at Hatfield, the day Parliament reconvened. The fall foliage was all but spent. An abundance of leaves was scattered all over the grounds. My workmen were raking them up and the pungent smell of them burning filled the air.

The skies were November gray. I drew my cloak around me as I dismounted from my horse. Cat and Mr. Parry and Roger Ascham came out to greet me. From the house kitchens I could smell good things cooking. The household dogs came out to greet me, to sniff everyone, and when one of my knights hailed another, the sound echoed off the empty trees in the front courtyard, where bushels of apples were lined up, red and inviting.

I was home.

For how long, I did not know. I wanted simply to sit in front of the fireplace in the front parlor and stare into the yellow and red flames. That first night I did. We had peace and contentment, all of us, while we roasted apples and nuts on the fire and drank hot mulled cider. My knights, Cat, Mr. Parry, and Roger—all of us—sat there bantering and making light talk, speaking of the horses in the stables, the cows in the barn, the fall harvest, and repairs that had been made on the roof.

Each knew, in our hearts, that this might be the last night we did this. That as soon as Mary died a certain formality would settle over us all. We were saying good-bye to something and hello to something else, we all sensed. But none of us were quite sure how it would be once I was Queen.

We waited. One week went by and once again messages were coming to Hatfield. Mary was declining. She had agreed there was no babe, no Prince. On the tenth of November five more heretics had gone to the stake at Canterbury.

"Let's hope those poor souls will be the last," I told Cat Ashley.

Other messages said that Mass was celebrated daily in Mary's bedchamber, that she had a ring sent to Philip to show him of her undying love. Still others said she had finally been convinced to make a will, making me her heir. Her only requirements were that I "keep the Roman Catholic faith in England and pay all her debts."

Cecil wrote to me privately saying that he was drafting proclamations announcing my accession to be sent to all the towns and shires.

Meanwhile, people were steadily coming to Hatfield. Every morning when I awoke I saw crowds of people at the gates come to serve me. They were peasants as well as noblemen. Because of the lean harvest and the plague of influenza, the peasants had to be fed and attended to.

Mr. Parry and Roger Ascham helped me with the problem. Together they investigated the noblemen and then hired them to help. The kitchen was going twenty-four hours a day to feed the hungry. I hired three more cooks. Roger Ascham fielded many requests for me.

Then came Sir William Cecil, riding up with an entourage of people to help me. He was to act as secretary, something he was very good at. And to advise and comfort.

We fed the hungry and gave them portions of food to take home. We hired some. We hired some dressmakers and tailors, even musicians and entertainers on the spot.

Some were sent to town to board; some were given rooms.

One man who came said he had the finest horses to sell. He brought one, a sleek animal who pranced and whinnied. I thought of Robin. I did not know horseflesh, but he would. I would need a Master of Horse. I looked for Robin but he did not come.

Pledges came of money and service, from knights vowing to set me on the throne or die beneath my banner.

A note came from Nicholas Throckmorton on the fifteenth, saying Mary was in a trancelike state, seeing angels, prone in bed and feverish, babbling in a dementia. She could not last the night.

I could not sleep that night. I had some of the hired musicians play soft music as I sat in the great room before the fire with my people and now Sir William Cecil. We waited up half the night. I fell asleep in my plush chair, clutching the carved lions' heads on the arms, and was aware only of someone putting a velvet cover over me, of taking off my velvet slippers and putting my feet on a footstool.

For a while I heard the soft talk of those around me and the music and the crackling of the fire. Then the talk and music stopped and I fell into a disturbed sleep. I dreamed I was back in the Tower, that the eight ravens were watching me with beady eyes, that little Henry Martin was handing me a bunch of ragged robin flowers.

Of a sudden I woke. The room was dark but for a few pine-knot torches set in wall sconces. Everyone was sleeping. John Chertsey was snoring. Mr. Parry and Sir William Cecil lay curled up on the Persian carpet on the floor. My knights were sprawled in chairs, completely oblivious of all that was about them. Cat Ashley was curled up on a couch and a few other servants sprawled about, all sleeping. I smiled.

This could be my last night as Princess. Tomorrow I could be Queen. My whole being surged with excitement and anticipation as I thought about it. I had wanted to be Queen since I was three and in a moment of childish fancy had made my knights kneel at my feet and declare me so.

I could not waste this night sleeping. Quietly I put on my slippers, took up my shawl, and stepped over people to go out into the hall, where guards were stationed. I gestured to the great wooden front door with the brass hinges and they nodded and opened it quietly for me.

Outside it was surprisingly warm for a November evening. The guards offered to follow me and I told them to keep a discreet distance. I wanted to be alone.

There was a three-quarter moon, and I walked across the front courtyard of Hatfield, feeling excited and warm and full of love for this place that had always taken me in when I was in trouble. Here I had lived as a toddler, when Cat Ashley had to scout up scraps of fabric to make my dresses because my father would not pay for any materials. Here I had ridden across the fields with Robin, just the two of us racing under the trees.

Here I had played with my poor little brother, who would grow up to be King and find himself pushed around by everyone. Here I had played with Lady Jane Grey, who had been Queen for only nine days and beheaded at sixteen. Here Mary had been sent to serve me when I was five or six, as punishment simply for being her mother's daughter, and here she would not kneel to me and we fought, even then.

Here I had studied and learned with my tutors, painstakingly conquering the problem of penmanship, so that now I could sign my name with flourishes and dignity and power.

I walked out of the courtyard to stand under an old holm oak, to lean and think. The eastern sky was already silver as if making ready for the sun. I heard a whinny of a horse from the barn, heard a dog bark, saw the guards in the distance standing and watching.

And then I heard them. A galloping of horses' hooves down the road, where trees and frightening shadows loomed. *They could be outriders,* I told myself, *here to plunder and steal.* But I knew they were not. Something about the urgency of the horses told me they were not. Robbers would approach quietly, not with a celebration of sound.

*How long,* I asked myself, as my eyes strained to see

them, *how long have you wanted to be Queen?* And the answer came. *All of my life.*

They were carrying torches. And they wore the green and white of the Tudor court. There were four of them from the Council. The first to dismount was Sir Nicholas Throckmorton.

He knelt at my feet. All the others dismounted and followed suit.

"The Queen is dead," said Throckmorton. "Long live the Queen."

I wanted to lean against the old oak for strength, but I must stand, straight and commanding. I must, until I must fall to my knees too, and say the verse I had so long practiced in private.

It was the Latin version of the 118th psalm. *"A Domine factum est illud et est mirabile in oculis nostris!"* I said. "This is the Lord's doing: it is marvelous in our eyes."

I rose and gestured that they should rise also. "Your Highness is being proclaimed in the House of Lords this morning," Sir Nicholas told me. "We could not wait for that." And he reached for my hand, which I gave him.

On my finger he put the black-and-gold coronation ring that Mary had worn to her death.

"Others are coming," Sir Nicholas said. "Clerks with books and records. Members of the court. You should go in, Your Majesty."

I turned to go, but halted. Others were coming out. Just

in time to see beacons flaring in the sky, to see bonfires lighted on the hills around Hatfield, to hear the bells of the local churches pealing.

"How news travels in this kingdom," Sir Nicholas said wryly.

My knights fell to their knees before me. Sir John Chertsey was crying. The Vernon brothers, who also had known me all my life, looked about to cry. Cat Ashley was babbling about gowns and jewelry, of getting out my red satin to wear this day. My maids hugged me. Mr. Parry was speaking in Welsh. Roger Ascham was quoting somebody in Greek. Sir William came out and knelt, and I immediately told him he was going to be my Secretary of State.

"Keep the people from the gates," Sir Nicholas yelled. Immediately my knights and yeomen were springing into action. I gave an order, and immediately my yeomen and some workers were bringing barrels and staves of wine from the cellar. The maids were bringing tankards and cider from the kitchen.

Then a new sound. The gallop of one horse in the distance, determined and rushing to me. It was light enough now for us to see him clear a fence in the pasture to take a shortcut. My heart stopped and I drew in my breath.

He came on a white horse, and dismounted even before the horse stopped. He fought his way through the crowd that had been slowly gathering at the gates, and his appearance alone warranted his entry.

He was dressed in green and white. A dark green doublet,

a green velvet cloak and jaunty hat, white trousers, black shining boots, and a silver-hilted sword at his side.

He swept off his hat and knelt before me. "Your Majesty," he said, "I am here to serve and congratulate you."

He handed me a bouquet of oak leaves as his pledge of love.

Tears were coming down his face.

I wanted to say, "Dear Robin, let's go riding across the fields and pick up the apples and walnuts from the ground." But I could not. Those days were over.

"I wanted to be the first to bring you the news, Majesty," he said breathlessly. "But these gentlemen"—he gestured toward Throckmorton and the other members of the council—"said it was not my place. They said—"

"You will have your place, Lord Robert Dudley," I told him. "I wish to make you my Master of Horse. What say you?"

He had been standing. Now he knelt again. "I will be happy to serve as your Master of Horse, Highness. I am at your service for anything."

Master of Horse! He knew what it meant. It meant he would be close to me. He would pick out the horse for me to ride every day. When we went anywhere, just out riding or in a procession to London, or on a royal progress, he would be right beside me.

He would be invited to court, attend all banquets and masques and tournaments and celebrations with me. My dear Robin!

"Now, Majesty," he said carefully, "I think, if I may make so bold, that you should go into the house. Kneeling at your feet, I could see that your slippers are wet through and through."

Everyone laughed and all went into the house to celebrate and to get to work for the kingdom.

# Author's Note

After writing some thirty-two novels concerning American history, why would I go outside my sphere of knowledge to write a book about Princess Elizabeth?

The only answer I have is the stock answer I call upon when being asked why I wrote any of my books: because she held my interest.

Because she sat there in the back of my mind and refused to leave, even as I explored the environment of Texas during the American Civil War and Georgia plantations before it.

Elizabeth just sat there on her gold-encrusted throne, surrounded by her knights; her ladies-in-waiting; her sickly brother, Edward, who was younger than she and already King of England; her half sister, Mary, who was ahead of her in line for the throne; the ghosts of her father, Henry VIII, and her mother, Anne Boleyn; and her dear friend Robin Dudley. And she waited.

She waited for me to finish fooling around with all my other duties and finally get to her. She had so much to tell me.

But hadn't she told it to so many others before? Weren't there numerous and wondrous books, fiction and nonfiction, about her trials, her comings and goings, her victories and her defeats?

She had, and there were. But she was always glad to tell her story again. There are as many versions of the princess's story as there are books about her, and as every writer does, I could not help but put my own interpretation on the life and adventures of this hearty, brave, noble soul who grew up to become Queen Elizabeth I.

I wasn't breaking any new ground in taking on England at this time. I had already written of Lady Jane Grey, so I knew of the language, the manners, the architecture of their minds, the foolishness of their loyalties, the impossibility of their dreams. I knew, for instance, that protocol dictated that no woman should go to the funeral of a King. That Elizabeth, though Henry VIII's daughter, dared not write him a letter directly. That because she was in line for the throne, to be caught kissing a man could be called treason and mean death for the unfortunate man and possibly for her.

I knew that though she might only be four years old, she would already have her own "household." That she could easily be removed from her place in line of succession to the throne at the mood of her father, and that one could be confined to the Tower for the mere suspicion of disloyalty.

Who would want to live in such a world? At its best it was primitive in the ways of justice; at its worst it was barbaric.

Ah, but if one was a noble, if one rubbed shoulders with royalty, one had moments of purest enjoyment in feasting, in clothing and adornment, in the numerous little courtesies of everyday life.

Did I do justice to the privileges awarded to persons of eminence? I could not possibly have, but it was a joy trying, a joy moving in and out of those chambers, under those sparkling chandeliers, beneath those tapestries and sculptures and past those knighted figures. Sitting down to dine with Henry VIII and little Elizabeth as he roars, "More wine, and a toast to my daughter!" Noting that small beret on his head with the feather that curls around his ears. Dancing with Sir Thomas Seymour, who was "loved by women and children and dogs throughout the kingdom." Being escorted by knights Richard and James Vernon through the great halls of the palace, the walls of which were painted with murals or hung with paintings of ancestors.

How did little Elizabeth learn to conduct herself in such surroundings? She was brought up to it by Cat Ashley, her first nanny, and later by her tutors. She was trained in manners and language. But it was only through her own strengths—inherited from her father, the King, and her mother, Anne Boleyn, who was executed—that she learned at an early age that all these trappings only hid dangers waiting to snare a Princess if she wasn't careful.

She learned at an early age—with the help of Cat Ashley, and her friend Robin Dudley, and Mr. Grindal, her tutor—to study hard and to think before speaking.

She learned that her father was King before he was her father. She learned what people would do to be King—and what she must and must not do to be Queen.

This novel is my own interpretation of Princess Elizabeth's struggle to grow up and be Queen of England. I am sure there are others more accurate, more intricate, and more exacting. I hope I succeeded in making mine interesting, eye-opening, and fun to read.

*Ann Rinaldi*

# BIBLIOGRAPHY

Dunn, Jane. *Elizabeth and Mary: Cousins, Rivals, Queens.* New York: Knopf, 2004.

Irwin, Margaret. *Elizabeth, Captive Princess.* London: Allison & Busby, 1999.

————. *Young Bess.* London: Allison & Busby, 1999.

Maxwell, Robin. *Virgin: Prelude to the Throne.* New York: Simon & Schuster, 2001.

Miles, Rosalind. *I, Elizabeth.* New York: Doubleday, 1994.

Plaidy, Jean. *Queen of this Realm: The Story of Elizabeth I.* New York: Putnam, 1985.

Starkey, David. *Elizabeth: The Struggle for the Throne.* London: Chatto & Windus, 2000.

Wagner, John A. *Historical Dictionary of the Elizabethan World: Britain, Ireland, Europe, and America.* New York:

Checkmark, 2002.

Weir, Allison. *The Children of Henry VIII*. New York: Ballantine, 1996.

————. *Henry VIII: The King and His Court*. New York: Ballantine, 2001.

————. *The Six Wives of Henry VIII*. New York: Ballantine, 1991.

4/08